KIDNAPPED!

As soon as the pistol shot exploded, Sue sat bolt upright in the bed. She knew that something was terribly wrong, but she didn't know what. Her first thought was for her daughter. She jumped out of the bed and ran toward the little room where Laurie slept, but a man grabbed her. She clawed at the man's face and screamed, twisting and struggling as hard as she could, but he was too strong for her. She knew she couldn't break his grip, so she bent her head to his shoulder and bit him. . . .

Laurie, too, was awakened by the gun blast. She sat up straight and called for her mother, but the words had hardly passed her lips before someone clapped a hand over her mouth and said, "Shut up, kid. Your uncle Angel is going to take you for a little ride."

Dell Books by Bill Crider

OUTRAGE AT BLANCO
TEXAS VIGILANTE

TEXAS VIGILANTE

BILL CRIDER

A DELL BOOK

Published by
Dell Publishing
a division of
Random House, Inc.
1540 Broadway
New York, New York 10036

ISBN: 0-440-23455-7

Printed in the United States of America
Published simultaneously in Canada
September 1999
10 9 8 7 6 5 4 3 2 1
OPM

This one is for
Scott Cupp.

PART 1

Chapter 1

By Angel Ware's reckoning, it had been two years, two months, and two days since he'd decided to kill Hob Bowman. He was beginning to think he was never going to get the chance.

Patience wasn't one of Angel's virtues. To tell the truth, he was pretty sure he didn't have any virtues at all. His mother had named him for his looks, not his nature. He had hair so blond that it was almost pure white, and eyes of such a light blue they might have been chips of ice, ice that could have been no colder or harder than Angel's heart.

Prison hadn't noticeably improved Angel's character, but he had at least learned a little about patience. What he'd learned, he didn't like, and it had only made him more impatient to kill Hob Bowman.

"Hob will be coming for you in a minute," Abilene Jack Sturdivant said, his voice as low and as flat as the Kansas prairie.

Abilene Jack sat on the floor with his back against the

stone wall and his knees drawn up under his chin. He had bad teeth and a bad disposition, and he was one of the two men with whom Angel shared a cell in the state prison at Huntsville.

The cell was five feet wide and seven feet long. It was hot and dark and it smelled like spoiled meat, unwashed bodies, and the contents of the slop bucket that sat back in the corner where Hoot Riley had thrown the carcass of the rat he'd killed earlier that morning.

Hoot Riley was the other occupant of the cell. He was quick with his hands, and he'd grabbed the rat and broken its neck quicker than a cat could lick its ass. Riley claimed that he was seventeen years old, but Angel didn't believe him.

There were plenty of kids in the prison who were younger than Hoot, and Angel didn't know why Riley claimed to be older than he was. He had red hair and freckles, and he probably wasn't much more than fifteen. But he was mean enough to be a hundred.

Hoot claimed to have killed three men, one of them with a hammer and the other two with a knife. Angel saw no reason to doubt him. He was quick enough with his hands to gut a man and then skin him out before he hit the ground.

"That Hob," Riley said. "He's a scutter."

"He's more than that," Angel said. "He's a lying bastard. One of these days I'll kill him."

"How?" Riley said, looking around the shadowy cell. "Hit him with a dead rat?"

Abilene Jack laughed softly and said to Angel, "After you ride the Horse awhile, you'll be a dead rat yourself."

Angel didn't like to think about the Horse. Bowman had put him on it more than once, and it was after the first time that Angel had decided to kill him.

Bowman, of course, had only been doing his job, but he'd enjoyed it too much to suit Angel. He'd smiled the whole damn time. It seemed like he was always smiling, but Angel was going to put a stop to that if he ever got the chance.

Someone in the next cell was moaning. There was nothing unusual abut that. It seemed like someone in the prison was always moaning, usually someone who'd been striped by Hob Bowman's bullwhip. Bowman was a man who enjoyed his job, all right. It was no wonder that he smiled so much.

"Here they come," Riley said.

On down the row, men were singing, coughing, talking, yelling, and crying. Angel didn't now how Riley could hear anyone coming, but Riley could hear a lot better than most people could.

"You going to put up a fight?" Abilene Jack asked Angel.

Angel didn't bother to answer. If he put up a fight, Bowman's trusties would just throw him down and beat him senseless.

Either that, or they'd kill him. Either way, it didn't matter much. They'd hoist him up on the horse, living or dead, and let him roast out there in the hot sun until they figured he was done. Then they'd take him down, carry him back inside, and throw him in the cell. If he was dead, they might take him back out in a day or two.

Or if they were feeling mean, which wasn't unlikely, they might leave him for a week. There wouldn't be much left of him by that time. Even Hoot, quick as he was, wouldn't be able to fight off all the rats that would come a-running.

Thinking about the Horse, Angel decided that being dead might not be so bad. He felt a phantom pain shoot through his shoulders and legs.

The Horse didn't look like much, just a thick post set in the ground, with a peg that could be moved up and down. The first time Angel saw it, he almost laughed in Hob Bowman's fat face to think that so many men feared it.

Then they'd set him up on the peg with his back to the post, tied his hands up high behind him, and started stretching his legs down. It wasn't too long before Angel knew that he wasn't nearly as tough as he'd thought he was.

His arms felt as if they were being torn from their sockets, and the pain in his legs was so intense that he almost screamed.

He didn't scream, however. He would have choked on his tongue before he gave Bowman that satisfaction. They left him up two hours before he passed out.

He'd ridden the Horse a couple of times after that, both times for minor infractions of the rules, infractions that were as much a creation of Bowman's imagination as real, just like the latest one. Whenever Bowman needed entertainment, he'd report Angel for some transgression against the rules, and up on the Horse Angel would go.

There was a loud clanging from down the row, and a harrowing scream ripped through the thick air. Someone had broken one of Bowman's rules, put his hand through the bars most likely, and one of the trusties had slammed it against the iron with the hickory club that he carried. The trusties, being prisoners themselves, delighted in using their special status to abuse their fellow inmates, something of a habit that Bowman encouraged. After the echo of the scream died away, Angel could hear Bowman's raucous laughter.

The trusty ran his club along the bars, making a *clong*-ing sound as he moved along the corridor.

"That Hob," Riley said again. "He does like to have a good time."

"So do you," Abilene Jack said.

Riley grinned. "Yeah. I don't blame the man."

"You would if it was you going up on the Horse," Angel said.

"Hob don't have it in for me like he does for you. What did you do to him, anyhow?"

"Nothing," Angel said. "Touched him up a little."

It had been more than that. The first time they put Angel in his cell, he'd broken Hob's nose, gotten in a solid smash with his elbow, and torn free of Hob's grip.

He'd been halfway down the corridor before the trusties caught him and clubbed him to the floor. He'd known he didn't have a chance of getting out of the prison, but it had been worth a try.

Or so he'd thought. The next day they put him up on the Horse and changed his mind.

"I am going to fight them," Angel said to Abilene Jack. "To hell with getting back on the Horse. Let 'em kill me if that's what they want to do."

Jack unfolded his legs and stood up. "Bastards can kill me, too, then. I've been in this place long enough. How about you, Hoot?"

Riley moved to the back of the cell to stand by the slop bucket and the dead rat.

"You fellas can do what you want to," he said. "I'm a young guy, and I'm plannin' on a long life after I get out of this place. Y'all go ahead and bust 'em up. I'll just watch from back here."

"Don't blame you none," Jack said, and Angel nodded.

"You can have the trusties," Angel told Jack. "Hob, though, he's mine."

Jack nodded. "You're welcome to him."

Hob and the two trusties reached the cell. Bowman was short and fat and sassy, a man who obviously ate much better than the prisoners. He was sweating profusely. He smelled worse that most of the prisoners, too.

A trusty stood on either side of him. They were at least a foot taller than Bowman, lean and hard as the hickory club that one of them carried.

A fourth man stood a good ten feet away. He was a

guard, and his name was Rankin. He wore a black patch over the place where his left eye had been. Angel had always heard that one-eyed men weren't very good shots, but that didn't matter in Rankin's case. He didn't use a pistol or a rifle. He carried a sawed-off shotgun.

According to stories that Angel had heard, Rankin had killed at least ten prisoners during his years at the prison. That was more men than Angel himself had killed, and sometimes he thought about the injustice of it all. The difference between him and Rankin was so small you couldn't slip a poker card in there, but the guard got to leave the prison anytime he wanted to.

Angel didn't pay any attention to Rankin or the trusties. He was looking at Bowman, and there was obviously something wrong, because Bowman wasn't smiling. Angel motioned to Jack to let him know that plans had changed. Something was going on, and maybe it wasn't the time to resist Bowman.

Jack nodded imperceptibly.

"This is your lucky day, Angel," Bowman said. He didn't sound happy about it.

"Why's that?" Angel asked.

"Because you're due to ride the Horse."

One of the trusties, a man everyone called Gut, smiled at Angel and swung his club into the palm of his hand, where it hit with a muted thud.

"What's so damned lucky about riding the Horse?" Angel asked.

"Not a thing," Bowman said. "The lucky thing is that you won't be riding after all. You've been assigned to a work detail."

Angel felt tension flowing out of his shoulders and back, but he didn't let his relief show. Or his surprise. He knew that prisoners in Texas were slaves of the state, and the state wanted its prisons to pay their own way. As a result, the prisons were run by private interests, and a great many of the prisoners worked on the plantations of private landowners. Convicted killers like Angel, however, were seldom allowed outside the walls.

Bowman obviously wasn't happy about the fact that Angel had been assigned outside work.

"There's a shortage of workers on the Fisher plantation," he said, looking as if he had a bad taste in his mouth and wanted to spit. "There's more to do there than we thought, and besides that, a couple of your friends made a run for it yesterday. Naturally the guards had to shoot 'em. Otherwise, we wouldn't be doin' this. I just hope *you* try to escape before we get you there. That would give me a chance to kill you."

Or me a chance to kill you, Angel thought, careful to keep his face free of all expression. It would be dangerous to let Bowman know the elation he was feeling.

"Riley and Sturdivant are going with you," Bowman said. "And Jephson."

Jephson was in the next cell. He was a thin man with narrow eyes who reminded Angel of a rattlesnake, except that Angel didn't think Jephson would give any warning before he struck. Angel had talked to him but didn't much like him, and he certainly didn't trust him. But then, he didn't much like or trust anybody.

"Sturdivant, you come out first," Bowman said, and Angel noticed for the first time that the trusty on Bowman's right, Yankee Tom, was carrying manacles.

Bowman unlocked the cell door with a heavy key and swung it open. The two trusties beside Bowman backed away so that Jack couldn't jump them. Rankin didn't move except to bring up the shotgun, ready to shoot if he had to.

Abilene Jack looked at Angel, who nodded. Jack stepped out the door, which Bowman relocked.

"Put your hands out," he said to Jack, who obeyed without speaking.

Yankee Tom locked on the manacles, which were linked by a short chain that also joined them to another pair of handcuffs.

"Now you, Riley," Bowman said, opening the door again.

Riley was locked into the manacles along with Jack. Then Jephson and Angel were cuffed together.

"We're gonna fix up your feet after we get you to the wagon," Bowman said. "I don't think you'll be doin' any running in here. Walk on along in front of us now, and don't take any chances. Rankin there doesn't have a thing against any of you, but if he had to take a shot, all four of you'd end up full of lead. Most likely one or two of you'd be dead, too. Maybe all of you, if justice was served."

Angel didn't say a word. He started walking. He gave a little jerk with his left hand, and Jephson came on along with him. Abilene Jack and Riley fell in behind them.

Angel wasn't going to take any chances on getting shot. Not there, not inside. All he could think of was that it had been two years, two months, and two days, but he was finally going to get his chance at Bowman.

And he was going to get it outside in the open air and sunshine. He hadn't seen sunshine in two years, except for the times they'd had him up on the Horse. It would be good to see it again.

It would be even better to kill Bowman. Angel could hardly wait.

Chapter 2

Ellie Taine listened to the rain drizzle on the roof, thinking that it had come just in time. The front had moved in from the west just before daylight, and it had been raining steadily ever since.

It had rained hard at first. It had pounded on the roof like mallets, so hard that it almost seemed as if it would break on through. It was coming down too hard to soak in the dry, cracked earth of the ranch, but that was all right. There would be other good results of the torrential downpour. Ellie imagined the nearly dry creeks and water holes filling up as the rainwater rushed in.

After about an hour, the rain had slowed down considerably. Now it would be penetrating the parched ground and getting down to the roots of the dying grass. In a day or so, the cattle would have plenty to graze on, with abundant water to drink besides. She wasn't going to lose any of them after all, or have to sell them for next to nothing, but it had been a near thing. Being the owner of a big ranch was just as hard and precarious a way of living as she'd thought it would be.

It wasn't as if she'd asked for it. Jonathan Crossland had given her the ranch and everything on it before he died, but he hadn't been able to leave her any money to get started or to take care of the place with. He'd told her that it would be up to her to handle that part.

She was trying her best, but she'd never owed anyone in her life. Now she found herself in debt to a bank in San Antonio and worried about making her payments on time. It wasn't a comfortable feeling, especially when rain was so chancy.

But Ellie was tough. The men who'd raped her and killed her husband a little more than a year before could have testified to that. If they'd been alive, that is.

They weren't alive, however, and the main reason for that was Ellie Taine. She'd gone out after them, and only one of them had lived to make the trip back to Blanco. He'd made the mistake of thinking that Ellie, being a woman, would rather let him escape than shoot him. It was the last mistake he ever made.

Ellie heard a knock on the door and started toward it, but Juana got there first. It was hard for Ellie to get used to having someone do things for her. Juana had worked for Jonathan, cleaned and cooked for him, and she had insisted on doing the same for Ellie. Unlike Jonathan, Ellie joined right in with her as often as not, sharing in all the housework. Juana had objected at first, but soon she'd seen that there was no way to keep Ellie from helping and given in with good grace.

The door opened, and Lane Tolbert came into the front room, rain dripping off his slicker. He and his family had come along several months after Ellie had inherited the ranch. He'd been looking for work, and Ellie had hired him at once, not just because he seemed to know something about ranching but because she liked his wife, Sue, and his daughter, Laurie. Especially Laurie.

Laurie was with Lane now, laughing as she shook rainwater off her hat. She was ten years old, with bright blue eyes and blond hair that seemed shinier than hair had a right to be. It was almost like sunlight in the room. Her mother's hair was the same.

There'd been a time when Ellie had wanted a child, but it hadn't happened. And Ellie knew she wasn't likely to get married again. She wasn't exactly the kind of woman men wanted for a wife. She was still young, but she'd been married once already, and she wasn't exactly a beauty. Even though she owned considerable property, no one had come courting her after her husband's murder.

Ellie didn't worry about things like marriage, however. With the ranch, she had plenty of other things to occupy her mind, and having Laurie around the place was almost as good as having a child of her own.

"Have you two had breakfast?" Ellie asked.

Laurie laughed again. "We get up real early, Miss Ellie. We had breakfast a long time ago."

"It wasn't that long ago," her father said, smiling. "But the way you eat, we have to get up early. Otherwise, you'd still be at the table all morning."

"I don't eat much," Laurie said, and Ellie smiled. "Just some eggs and bacon." She looked at her father. "And you wouldn't let me have any coffee."

"Well, we didn't come here to talk about food," Lane said. He looked at Ellie. "I'd better go check on that low place down behind the cottonwoods. We've had a lot of water, and a place like that gets muddy mighty fast. We don't want any cattle to get bogged down there. And if they're already stuck, we'd better get 'em out."

"That's fine," Ellie said. "Take one of the other hands with you. What about Laurie?"

Lane turned his hat in his hands. "I hate to ask it, but would you mind if she stayed with you for a while? Her ma's got a touch of something."

Ellie stopped smiling. "Does she have a fever?"

"Not much of one. She's just feeling peaked. If you could look in on her later, I'd sure appreciate it."

"Well, Laurie's certainly welcome to stay with me." Ellie was secretly pleased. She always enjoyed having the child around. "And I'll be glad to look in on Sue. Laurie and I can read some more of that book by Mr. Irving before we go."

"About Rip Van Winkle?" Laurie asked.

Ellie shook her head. "We've read that one already."

"We could read it again."

"Well, I guess we could, at that."

Ellie enjoyed reading aloud to the girl, and it didn't matter to her if the story was one that she'd read already, especially if Laurie liked it.

"How much longer do you think the rain will last?" Ellie asked Lane.

"Maybe an hour or so. It's already getting light back in the west. I never heard a harder one, though. It did us some good."

He turned to go out the door. Laurie was already heading to the big room that first Jonathan Crossland and now Ellie used as an office. Jonathan had kept his library in there, too, several thick, heavy books in a tall bookcase.

Ellie had been reading some of the books in the evenings when she had time. She liked the ones by Irving and Cooper, but she wasn't as fond of the ones by Melville and Hawthorne. She liked Shakespeare, too, but she wasn't sure that Laurie was ready for something like that.

Laurie was awfully smart, though, smart as a whip. She might just catch on to that Shakespeare fellow without much trouble at all. And besides being smart, Laurie had plenty of spirit. She liked to laugh and joke, and she stood up for herself when she thought she was in the right. She was just the kind of girl that Ellie would have wanted for a daughter if she'd ever had one. She never would, though, so she would just have to enjoy Laurie, who, Ellie told herself, would be around the place for years to come.

Smiling at the thought, Ellie followed Laurie into the office.

Chapter 3

Hob Bowman didn't like the situation one bit. Letting Angel work outside the Walls was a bad idea from the git-go, but the warden had said it had to be done, and the warden was the man who ran things. Mr. Fisher needed men, the warden said, and Angel Ware was as able-bodied a man as there was in the whole prison. Sturdivant, Riley, and Jephson weren't far behind. Besides, according to the warden, Ware wasn't any worse than any of the rest of the bad 'uns they had locked up, and he was probably better than some.

Which proved to Bowman that the warden didn't know diddly-squat about the prisoners. As far as Bowman was concerned, Ware was the worst son of a bitch behind bars in the state of Texas. He'd known it since the first day that Ware had turned up at Huntsville and broken Bowman's nose. If it had been up to Bowman, Ware would have been dead and buried out behind the prison in an unmarked grave a long time ago.

Well, maybe he could do something about that now. There wasn't much doubt in his mind that Ware would try something on the way to the Fisher plantation. That's just the way Ware was, and Bowman aimed to take advantage. In fact, he was going to help Ware out. He'd give Ware a little opening, and when Ware took it, Bowman would be ready for him. He'd already had a little talk with Rankin about the way it would go.

And if any of the others tried to help Ware out, well, that was too bad for them. Bowman would just as soon have them dead, too. They were troublemakers, all of them. There was no way the warden could blame Bowman for having them shot, not if they were trying to escape. The prison orders were clear on that point. Shoot to kill. There'd been far too many escapes in the last year or so, and it was beginning to look bad on the warden's record.

Bowman had to admit that the prisoners in the wagon didn't look like they felt up to escaping. They were manacled together two by two at the wrists and ankles, and while they might be able to get out of the wagon, they weren't going to shuffle very far away before they got ripped apart by the shotgun. Bowman knew what kind of hole Rankin's gun could make in a man. He'd seen it more than once. It was big enough to drive a steam locomotive through.

Bowman had called Yankee Tom and Gut aside

earlier and explained that the prisoners were most likely going to make a break for it.

"And Rankin'll have to kill 'em," he said. "We can't have any escapes. It's bad for discipline. You can see that, can't you."

"Sure can, boss," Gut said. "You can't let those bastards get away. No tellin' what they might do to the citizens if they was on the loose. And we sure wouldn't want anybody else gettin' ideas."

Yankee Tom just nodded. He was a man who didn't like to waste any more time talking than was absolutely necessary.

The thing Bowman hadn't counted on was the rain. The day had been hot and clear when they started out, so hot that Bowman had felt as if he might boil in his own sweat.

Then the clouds started to pile up, big and thick and fluffy white on top, but with flat black bottoms. After that, it began to get dark back to the north and west. The wind began to pick up a little just after noon. Dust danced along the wagon tracks, and little grains of sand jumped up off the ground to sting Bowman on the face.

"Storm comin', looks like," Gut said.

Yankee Tom nodded.

"Bad one, from the looks of it," Gut said. "And we're gonna be caught out in the open unless we can make that stand of pines."

The trees that Gut was referring to were about a

mile ahead, in the direction of the storm. Bowman didn't think the pines were likely to provide much cover, but he supposed they'd be better than nothing. And once in the trees, he might be able to tempt Ware to try an escape.

That's what he'd been planning to do all along, get back in the trees, out of sight of anyone who might happen along, and let Rankin take care of business.

Bowman was driving the team of mules, and Rankin was sitting beside him on the wagon seat, looking back at the prisoners every now and again, turning that one eye on them without saying a word. He didn't talk even as much as Yankee Tom.

Bowman shook the reins, but the mules weren't much encouraged. They seemed to sense the approaching storm. Probably smelled it, Bowman thought, and they didn't want to head into it.

Bowman's bullwhip was lying on the seat between him and Rankin, but he didn't pick it up. He used it on the prisoners every day without a second thought, but he didn't like to use it on animals. The mules plodded on at their own pace.

"We ain't gonna make it," Gut said, as the wind picked up.

Ahead of them the trees were bending under the force of an even stronger wind. In the dark clouds there was a bright white flash, and then the thunder rolled. A few big drops of rain spattered into the wagon.

The mules picked up their pace, as if they had decided that Gut was right about getting to the cover of the trees, but they were still a hundred yards away when the storm hit.

Bowman could hear it coming through the trees, the water sounding like a billion agitated bees as it slashed down through the green needles of the pines, the wind whipping through the branches. After that it was only seconds before a powerful wind hit them, ripping off Rankin's black hat and sending it flying away like a carrion crow. Then a wall of water washed over the wagon.

Angel drank it in. No one had given the prisoners anything to drink before they'd started out, and Angel hadn't had a bath in two years. He turned up his face and let the rain batter him. It ran through his hair and soaked his ragged prison clothes. It was falling so hard that it almost bruised his forehead and flattened his eyeballs behind his closed lids. The raindrops rattled off the wagon bed like gunshots. Lightning flashed again, and thunder grumbled.

Bowman was cursing the mules as the wagon slewed in the suddenly muddy road, but his voice was lost in the rush of the rain. Water swirled around the wagon wheels, and the wagon slipped sideways, then slid back on track.

Gut and Yankee Tom were thrown off balance, and Angel might have risked jumping them then if he'd been ready. He didn't think it would have worked, though, because he was manacled to Jephson, who didn't look as if he was ready for anything. He was bending double, making a futile effort to keep some part of himself dry in the battering storm.

Riley and Sturdivant were looking at Angel, who shook his head. If they were going to try anything at all, they'd have to wait for a better chance.

The wagon reached the trees. Mist rose up off the ground like smoke. The rain sluiced off the pine needles in tiny waterfalls, but its force was reduced. When they had gotten about thirty yards into the thicket, Bowman slowed the wagon to a stop. There was no one around, and no one was likely to come along.

"I think there's something wrong with one of the wheels," Bowman said. "Feels loose to me. I want you boys to get out and have a look at it."

Gut and Yankee Tom climbed out of the wagon. They held their clubs loosely and stood in the rain as if waiting for something to happen.

Angel had a pretty good idea what the something was.

"I didn't mean just them boys," Bowman said. "I meant you, Ware. You and Jephson and Riley and Sturdivant. Y'all get on out now and have a look at that wheel."

Angel wiped water from his face and turned his icy blue gaze first on Bowman and then on Rankin. But he didn't make any move to get up. Jephson started to stand, and Angel jerked on the manacles, bringing Jephson back down to the wagon bed.

"I know the kind of a man you are, Bowman," Angel said, raising his voice so he could be heard over the sound of the rain. "And since I know you, we're not going any damned where. If you're thinking about having your butt-boy kill us, he'll have to do it while we're sitting right here."

Bowman didn't make any attempt to deny what his plan was. He knew Ware wouldn't believe him anyway.

"You know something, Ware?" Bowman said, touching his nose as if it were tender. "You've been a trouble to me ever since you came behind the Walls. You tried to escape your first day, and I should've killed you then. But I didn't. I don't know why. It was just a mistake, and now I'm going to take care of it."

"There'll be blood and buckshot all over the wagon bed," Angel said. "It might be hard to explain that to the warden when you get back. Not many people try to escape while they're sittin' down in a wagon."

"This rain'll wash out any blood there is," Bowman said. "Poorly as you fellas look, there won't be too much of it. Gut and Yankee Tom can pick the buckshot out. So you can die sittin' there, or you can die on your feet like a man. It's up to you. I don't give a damn, and neither does Rankin. Ain't that right Rankin?"

Rankin nodded. His thin black hair hung in wet strings around his face.

"Hell, Angel, let's get out of the wagon," Abilene Jack said, leaning forward. "I don't much give a damn whether they shoot us or not. If they do, at least we won't have to go back to that damn prison."

"Damned if I'm gettin' shot," Hoot said. "I'm too young and pretty to die. If you get out, you'll have to carry me."

"Ain't worth the trouble, then," Jack said. He relaxed against the side of the wagon.

Bowman sighed. "That's fine with me, boys, if that's the way you want it. Just remember that I gave you a chance to die standin' up. Shoot 'em, Rankin."

Rankin raised the shotgun, Jephson screamed, and lightning struck a pine tree not ten feet away.

Chapter 4

It was as if a stick of dynamite had exploded in the tree, which shattered into a thousand pieces, throwing limbs and splinters everywhere. Sparks flew upward like fireflies and were snuffed out by the rain.

One of the tree limbs, a short one, maybe two feet long, broke off and tore straight through Yankee Tom's chest. The limb was as hard and white as bone, except where it was stained by Yankee Tom's blood.

Yankee Tom stood flat-footed for just a second, never making a sound, though his mouth was wide open. He had his hands around the part of the limb that stuck out in front of him, as if he might be going to pull it out and toss it aside.

Then he fell on his face without a word. Gut knelt beside him, screaming something that Angel couldn't hear because his ears were ringing and because the mules had bolted straight ahead, nearly throwing the prisoners out of the wagon.

The mules had, in fact, tossed Bowman and Rankin

off the seat in front, and now the mules were running free while the prisoners bounced around in the wagon bed like corn-shuck toys.

"Get up, goddammit!" Angel yelled at Jephson while he tried to stand himself. "We've got to stop those mules!"

Angel crawled over the jouncing wagon bed, which was slick and wet as a river rock, dragging Jephson along with him. When he got to the front, he pulled himself up and saw that he wasn't going to be able to reach the reins. They flopped out over the mules' backs like black ribbons in the wind.

He also saw that the wagon was going to stop soon anyway. The mules weren't running in the road, and there were trees all around.

That was Angel's last thought before the wagon wheels on the left side hit something—a log, a rock, a hole—Angel never knew just what, and it didn't matter.

The wagon flew up, turned halfway over, and dumped the prisoners out just before it slammed into a tree trunk with a crack like thunder.

Angel found himself rolling in the mud with Jephson dragging on him like an anchor. The rain washed over them like a river.

Angel tried to stand and slipped back into the mud. Jephson was just lying there. He was alive, though. Angel could see him breathing.

Angel was tempted to kill him right there where he lay, mash his face down into the mud and let him strangle on it, but Angel knew he couldn't do that. He needed

Jephson alive as long as they were manacled together. He sure as hell couldn't carry him.

He looked around. Jack and Hoot were lying in the mud, looking dazed. Jack's face was bleeding, and a pale splinter was sticking out of Hoot's left arm halfway between the elbow and the shoulder.

Angel didn't have time to worry about that. He had his own problems. He got to his knees and slapped Jephson across the mouth.

"Stand up, you son of a bitch." His voice seemed to echo around his head. "Rankin'll be here with that shotgun before you know it. We have to get away from here."

Something about that seemed to register with Jephson. He shook his head, blinked, and bent forward. Angel dragged him up into a sitting position, then stood himself. Jephson came along with him.

"Come on," Angel said, pulling Jephson toward where Jack and Hoot lay.

They hobbled over to stand above the prone prisoners. Jack looked up at them. Hoot was moaning softly with his eyes closed.

"Hoot's hurt," Jack said.

"I can see that," Angel said. "He's gonna be hurt a lot worse if Rankin blasts him with that scattergun of his. Can you get up?"

"Sure enough," Jack said. "Come on, Hoot, boy."

Jack stood, bringing Hoot up with him. Hoot opened his eyes and looked at his arm.

"Got a damn pine limb stuck in me," he said.

Angel looked at it. There wasn't much blood. "Might just be part of the wagon. We'll see about it later on. Right now, we gotta get away from Rankin and that bastard Bowman."

"Maybe they got their necks broke," Jephson said hopefully.

"We ain't that lucky," Jack said.

"Maybe we are," Angel said. "Else they'd be after us by now."

"They are after us," Hoot said, his keen hearing apparently undisturbed by the rushing rain, the explosion, or the fall.

He pointed through the blanket of rain with his undamaged right arm. Angel could see two dark figures moving toward them. He wondered if they could see him.

Maybe not.

"Let's move off into the trees," he said. "We might can get behind them and catch them off guard."

He didn't know exactly how that was going to be possible, but it was worth a try. And it was a hell of a lot better than standing around out there in the rain waiting for Rankin to kill them.

He stumbled away, hauling Jephson along. He didn't look to see if Jack and Hoot were coming. If they did, that was fine. If they didn't, that was their own lookout.

When he had gone twenty or so yards to the left, he turned to where he guessed Rankin and Bowman would be. He yanked the chain to get Jephson's attention and put his finger to his lips. Jephson nodded, and they started working their way back toward the wagon track.

Angel had no real idea where Bowman and Rankin might be at the present, however. The rain was still coming down hard. Everything was blurred. He looked back to see if Hoot and Jack were behind them.

They were, and Angel motioned for them to catch up. When they did, he put his mouth near Hoot's ear.

"Where the hell are they?" he said.

Hoot didn't hesitate. He pointed off through the trees, and Angel thought he could make out two dim silhouettes through the haze of falling water.

The sky flashed white, and for less than a second Angel had a clear view of Bowman and Rankin slinking through the trees. Then it was dark and thunder crashed above them.

"We'll come up behind them," he said. He was pretty sure that neither Bowman nor Rankin could hear half as well as Hoot. "Bowman's mine. Jack, you and Hoot will have to take care of Rankin and that sawed-off greener of his. Can you do it?"

Hoot held out his left arm. "I'm not sure. This thing hurts like hell."

"This is gonna hurt even worse," Angel said. "Don't make a damn sound."

Angel grabbed the splinter with both hands, Jephson's hands coming awkwardly along. Hoot's mouth opened, then clapped shut as he bit off the yell before it escaped.

"You ready?" Angel asked.

Hoot's eyes were wide, but he kept his mouth resolutely shut as he nodded.

Angel yanked out the splinter. Blood gushed out with it and swirled away in the rain. Hoot slumped, but Jack held him up.

"Goddamn," Hoot said, shaking his head. "Goddamn."

Angel waited for a ten-count. Then he said, "Let's go get 'em."

Chapter 5

Ellie and Laurie were finished with the reading. Laurie had been quite taken with the story about the skinny schoolteacher named Ichabod Crane and his amusing encounter with the Headless Horseman.

"Can we read it again?" she asked. "It's even better than the one about Rip Van Winkle."

Ellie closed the book and put it back on the shelf. She'd enjoyed the story, too, but she didn't want to read it again so soon.

"There are other stories in the book," she said. "We'll read some of those, and then we'll read about Mr. Crane again. But not today."

"Can I read it to you, then?"

Ellie knew that Laurie could read well, but she didn't think the child's skills were quite up to tackling the words of Mr. Irving.

"We should go look in on your mother," Ellie said.

Laurie shook her head impatiently. "Oh, she's all right. She just didn't sleep good."

"All the more reason we should see about her. What would you like for lunch? I'll speak to Juana before we go."

The thought of lunch took Laurie's mind off reading. She skipped a step or two around the room and said, "Fried steak. Can we have fried steak? And peas? And potatoes?"

Ellie laughed. "I'll see."

She went into the kitchen with Laurie tagging along behind and told Juana that Laurie would be joining them for lunch. Juana said that she would be glad to fry some steak and mash some potatoes.

"And peas," Laurie said. "Don't forget the peas."

"And peas," Juana said. "*Bueno.*"

Ellie told her to fix enough for Sue Tolbert. "She might not feel like eating much," Ellie said, "but I'm going to ask her to come up here and eat with us anyway."

"*Bueno,*" Juana said.

Ellie and Laurie went out the back door into the sunshine that had replaced the darkness and rain. The sky was washed a brilliant blue, and there wasn't a cloud to be seen.

Ellie stopped for a moment to enjoy the view, then turned toward the small foreman's house, which had never been lived in until Lane Tolbert and his family had moved in. Jonathan Crossland had never had a use for it. He'd been the ramrod of his own spread, but Ellie hadn't wanted to take on that job for herself. She was grateful that the house was there. Tolbert had said that it was just what he was looking for.

There was a small bunkhouse as well, where Ellie's

hired hands lived. Crossland had hired men when he needed them, but he'd never had a permanent crew.

Laurie ran on ahead of Ellie, not being as careful as Ellie to avoid the puddles and the worst of the mud. She made a meager attempt at wiping off her shoes, then opened the door and ran into the house. Ellie could hear her calling for her mother.

Ellie went inside. There was no one in the front room, but Ellie could see into the tiny kitchen, where Sue Tolbert sat at the table, trying to smile at her daughter, who danced around her, telling her all about Ichabod Crane.

". . . and there was big man named Bones, and he was big and strong, and . . ."

Ellie came into the kitchen, and Sue looked up.

"You can tell me about it later, Laurie," she said. "I'll bet Miss Ellie already knows the whole story."

"She ought to," Laurie said. "She read it to me."

"And did you thank her?"

"Maybe. I don't remember. Thanks, Miss Ellie."

"You're welcome," Ellie said. Then to Sue she said, "Your husband said you weren't feeling well today."

Sue shook her head, and her bright blond hair danced. "I hope he didn't worry you about me. I'm not sick. I just had a bad night. I tossed and turned and didn't sleep much. It's nothing. Just bad dreams."

"I have bad dreams sometimes," Laurie said. She looked thoughtful. "But I don't remember them now."

Ellie knew all about bad nights and bad dreams. She'd

had more than her share in the last year or so. Even worse, she could remember them.

"Do you remember yours?" she asked Sue.

Sue didn't meet Ellie's eyes.

"They were just silly dreams," she said.

Ellie pulled out a straight-backed wooden chair and sat down. She rested her arms on the table and said, "Dreams aren't always silly. My grandmother used to believe they could tell the future."

It wasn't the right thing to say. Sue's face crumpled, and for a second Ellie thought Sue might be going to cry.

Laurie tugged on her mother's dress. "Don't cry," she said. "It was just an old dream. Dreams aren't real. Remember? You told me so."

Sue composed herself. "Of course I remember. I was being silly, wasn't I?"

"Yes, you were," Laurie said sternly.

"I won't do it again."

"Promise?"

"I promise," Sue said. "Now, why don't you go clean some of that mud off your shoes and let me and Miss Ellie have a little talk."

"All right," Laurie said, running out the back door to the small covered porch, where she sat and began removing her shoes.

"The dreams worried you, didn't they," Ellie said.

Sue nodded. "But that's just being silly, as I told Laurie."

"What were they about?"

"Just some things that happened a long time ago. They're nothing. Really."

"They were about things that are still worrying you, weren't they," Ellie said.

"Not so much now that it's daylight. Those things always seem much worse at night."

Ellie knew all about that. Sometimes she woke up all in a sweat after dreaming that she was lying in the back of a wagon with a man named Ben Atticks about to rape her. It had been bad enough the first time, when it had really happened. Reliving it so vividly in the early hours of the morning was somehow even worse.

"It was probably all that thunder and lightning," Sue went on. "Things like that can cause dreams, you know. I don't much like storms."

"We needed this one," Ellie said. "Or we needed the water it brought. Sometimes good can come out of bad."

She thought about Jonathan Crossland and the friendship that had grown up between them. It had been a fine thing, though short-lived, and it would never have come into being if not for all the bad things that surrounded it.

"That doesn't change the bad things," Sue said. "You never forget them."

"No," Ellie agreed. "You never do."

She considered herself an expert on that topic, but she'd never discussed it with Sue. For that matter, Sue had never discussed much about her past with Ellie.

"Would you like to talk about your dreams?" Ellie asked.

"I'm not sure," Sue said. She stared up at the ceiling for a few seconds, then said, "Did you ever have a brother?"

Ellie shook her head. "I'm an only child."

"Consider yourself blessed," Sue told her.

Chapter 6

—◆—◆—

Angel told Jephson what they were going to do. Bowman was lagging a little behind Rankin. They'd get as close to Bowman as they could and then jump him while Jack and Hoot took on Rankin.

"You think you can jump when I tell you to?" he asked Jephson.

Jephson's clothing was plastered to him by water and mud. He looked like a drowned rat, incapable of any action at all, but he said he thought he could do it.

"You'd damn well better," Angel said. He held up his hands. "Just let me get this chain around his neck and my knee in his back. You try to keep out of the way."

Jephson nodded, but getting close to Bowman wasn't going to be easy. The manacles made walking difficult at best, and walking quietly was almost impossible. The noise didn't make much difference, however. It was almost impossible to hear anything over the roar of the wind and the rain.

They got to within two yards of Bowman before something warned Rankin, who turned to look behind him.

Angel didn't wait to see what happened.

"Now!" he said, and sprang for Bowman, who was so slow to react that he still hadn't turned.

Jephson came right along, and Angel landed on Bowman's back. Bowman pitched forward, and Angel looped the chain around his neck before they hit the ground.

There was a shotgun blast off to the left, but Angel paid it no mind. He landed on Bowman's back and felt the breath go out of the fat guard. He braced his knee on Bowman's spine and yanked back on the chain.

The shotgun blasted again, but it had no effect on Angel, who continued to put the pressure on Bowman's neck.

Bowman thrashed under Angel, kicking his legs and flailing his arms. Angel locked his legs around Bowman's broad middle and refused to be thrown aside. He pulled back even harder on the chain. Bowman started to make a wet cawing sound, and his hands tore futilely at the chain that was sunk in the folds of his neck.

Angel laughed and gave a hard jerk backward. Something in Bowman's neck popped like a broken branch. Bowman shuddered and collapsed facedown in the mud.

Angel unlooped the chain and looked to his right. Over Jephson's head he could see Rankin struggling with Hoot and Jack. There was no sign of the shotgun.

"Let's go help the boys out," Angel said to Jephson.

They stood up, and Angel kicked Bowman's limp body.

"Bastard," he said.

He would have spit on him, but with all the rain it would have been a wasted effort.

"Let's see if he was the one carrying a key to these manacles," Angel said.

He and Jephson bent down and searched through Bowman's clothing. They found the keys in his coat pocket. Angel didn't waste any time in getting free.

"Not let's see about that bastard Rankin," he said.

He and Jephson ran toward Rankin, who was struggling on the ground in a tangle with Hoot and Jack, who had been unable to get the chair around Rankin's neck.

The shotgun was lying uselessly a yard or so away from the struggle, so Angel picked it up by the double barrel. He waited until Rankin's head was clear of the tangle and then clubbed the guard on the back of the skull.

Rankin collapsed like an empty bag. Angel waited until Hoot and Jack had squirmed out from under him and then hit him again. Water drops flew off Rankin's hair, and his skull crushed like the shell of a terrapin hit with a rock. Rankin shuddered all over. Then he was still.

"Let me have a turn at the son of a bitch," Hoot said as he got to his feet. "I thought for sure he was gonna kill us."

"He didn't even get a shot at us," Jack told Angel. "I had ahold of the gun. He fired in the air a couple of times while I was trying to take it away from him. He got in a pretty good lick on me before he dropped it, too."

There was a bruised lump on Jack's forehead, but it

didn't look too bad. It would look worse later, Angel thought.

"What now?" Jack asked.

"Now we get you out of those chains," Angel said, tossing Jephson the keys.

While Jephson was freeing the others, Angel bent down to Rankin's body. The guard had a belt full of shotgun shells looped over his shoulder. Angel lifted Rankin's right side, slipped Rankin's arm through the belt, and pulled it off. Then he looped it over his own shoulder.

"Is he still breathing?" Hoot asked.

"Not so's you'd notice," Angel said. "No use to waste good buckshot on him."

He took two shotgun shells from the belt and broke the shotgun. He inserted the shells and snapped the gun back together.

"Let's go see what Gut's up to," he said.

The four men slogged through the mud and rain to where Gut was still kneeling beside Yankee Tom. Gut looked up and saw them, but he didn't move from where he was.

Angel bent down and picked up Gut's hickory club, then handed it to Jephson. Jack got the club that had belonged to Yankee Tom.

Angel pointed the shotgun at Gut and said, "Gut, you sorry son of a bitch, you've pounded on your last prisoner."

Gut looked up at him, rain streaming off his face. His eyes were red, and Angel thought he must have been crying.

"You can shoot me if you want to," Gut said. "I don't

give a damn. Yankee Tom's dead, and I might just as well be dead, too."

"So that's the way it was," Angel said.

"You can go to hell," Gut said.

"You first," Angel said, and pulled one of the triggers.

There was a sound as loud as the thunder, and the heavy buckshot tore away half of Gut's chest. For a second the rain around Gut was hazed with red.

"Some fun!" Hoot said.

"It's not fun," Angel said. "It's just necessary. Let's go see if we can catch those jugheads."

"I don't like the idea of ridin' a mule," Hoot said. "It's not dignified, and they'd just as soon kick you as look at you. Besides, they're bad about bitin'."

"Talk to him, Jack," Angel said.

"A mule's a whole lot better than a horse in some ways," Jack said. "Smarter, steadier, and a lot harder worker. You don't need to be ashamed of riding a mule."

Hoot looked skeptical, then smiled. "As long as I'm ridin', I don't much care. What about my arm?"

"It's just a scratch," Angel said. "We'll bandage it up as best we can. It's going to bleed a little, but there's not a damn thing we can do about that."

"Where do we go from here, then?" Hoot asked.

"We can split up if that's what you want," Angel said. "Or we can stick together for a while and see what turns up."

"I been inside a long time," Hoot said. "I'd like to kill somebody, burn down a barn or two, pay those bastards back for putting me in that goddamn place. What about you?"

"Me?" Angel said. He pushed his streaming hair back out of his face. "Me, I think I'll pay a visit to my family."

Chapter 7

— ·∗· —

"My brother was a beautiful child," Sue Tolbert said. "That's why my mother named him Angel."

Sue and Ellie were sitting at the round wooden table in the main ranch house, having just finished the lunch prepared by Juana. Laurie was in Ellie's office, paging through some of the books and reading what she could. She couldn't hear what the adults were saying. Otherwise, Sue would never have been willing to discuss her brother.

"He had the finest blond hair," Sue said. "It flew all around his head like floss. And blue eyes, light, pale blue. He even had dimples when he smiled. To see him, you'd think he'd just dropped down from heaven."

"I guess he didn't, though," Ellie said.

"No, he didn't. The way he was and the way he looked didn't match up. If he came from anywhere, it wasn't heaven. Just the opposite, maybe. But we didn't know that at first. He was just like any other baby, only prettier. I was five years old when he was born, and I thought he was the best thing that had ever happened. It was like having a new doll to play with, only better." Sue's eyes got a faraway look. "I can still remember our mother singing to him when she sat in the rocker and held him."

Ellie thought that was a nice memory. She didn't have any brothers or sisters, and she didn't remember much about her own childhood. What she remembered mostly had to do with working. She didn't remember any singing at all.

Sue's eyes closed, and she hummed a few bars of some half-forgotten lullaby.

"I can't remember any more of it than that," she said, opening her eyes and smiling faintly. "That was a good time, though, when Angel was just a little baby and before the bad things started happening."

Ellie wasn't sure she wanted to hear about the bad times. She'd had plenty of those herself. But she could tell that Sue wanted to talk, and maybe it would do her some good.

So she said, "What kind of bad things?"

"Angel started to kill animals," Sue said. "It was before he was even six years old. I saw him outside one day, chunking rocks at something on the ground. When I went out, I saw that it was a horned frog. He'd flattened it out good and proper, and there was blood all mixed in with the dirt, but he was still chunking at it. I tried to make him stop, and he started throwing rocks at me instead."

"I'll bet your daddy didn't like that," Ellie said, remembering her own father, who could be insensitive in many ways but who had been fiercely protective of his only child.

Sue extended her arms onto the table and clasped her fingers, as if trying to stop her hands from trembling.

"My father wasn't there. He worked for the railroad and wasn't home a lot, and when he was home, we didn't see much of him. He was in the saloon more often than in the house. My mother tried to stop Angel that day, but that just made him angrier. I think he hated me from that moment on."

"Did he ever hurt you?"

Sue unclasped her fingers and brushed at her eyes with her right hand. Then she put her hands in her lap.

"No," she said. "He never hurt me." She paused. "He tried, though."

Ellie was certain she didn't want to hear more. The look in Sue's eyes made it clear that the story was a painful one. But Sue was going to tell it.

"Angel killed other animals later on. He killed a neighbor's dog once, strangled it with a rope. He said he didn't do it, but we knew he did. The neighbor knew it too, but there wasn't anything he could do about it. And Angel picked fights with all the boys at school, even the ones that were bigger than he was. If he got whipped, he always got even. He'd wait till the boy who whipped him was off guard, maybe catch him on the way home from school some afternoon, and then he'd use a stick or a rock on him. There was one boy, John Temple, that was hurt the worst. Angel jabbed him in the face with a sharp stick and put his eye out. I knew what happened, and I told our parents. They were afraid to punish Angel by that time, afraid of what he might do to them, but they didn't make him go back to school. I'm sure everyone was happy about that, especially the other boys."

"What about you?" Ellie asked, certain that she would be sorry she asked. "What did he try to do to you?"

"Oh, he tried to kill me," Sue said, almost matter-of-factly. "He waited a long time, so long that I'd almost forgotten that I was the one who'd told about John Temple. I would've thought he'd forgotten too, but that was another thing about Angel. He never forgot anything that anyone did to him, not ever. He always said that sooner or later he'd get anyone who did him a bad turn. Usually it was sooner, but he never got a chance with me until later. My mother watched him too closely, I guess. But then she forgot, too, and Angel came after me one night with a stick of dry kindling about two feet long. It was round and solid and hard as a rock."

She looked at Ellie, then looked away. "I was in bed asleep. It was dark in the room, or he would have killed me, most likely. As it was, he swung where he thought my head was on the pillow and just barely grazed me. I woke up and rolled over, so he missed me completely the second time. My mother came in with a lamp, and he swung at her. He hit her in the knee, and she fell. She dropped the lamp, and it shattered."

Sue looked out the window. Her lower lip was trembling slightly, but her eyes were completely dry and her voice was steady.

"The next thing I knew the bed was on fire. I jumped up, and Angel swung at me again. He hit me that time, hard, right on the arm, and my whole arm just went numb. I stood there and watched him hit my mother in the head with that stick, and I couldn't even try to take it away from him."

"You don't have to tell me any more," Ellie said.

Sue shook her head. "I want to. I've never told anybody about this except Lane, but you've treated us so well and been so kind to Laurie that you deserve to know."

Ellie wasn't sure why she deserved anything, much less a story like the one that was unfolding.

"Are you telling me all this because of your dreams?" she asked.

Sue looked uncertain. "Maybe that's a part of it. They were bad dreams, and I've had them before. They're always the same. I dream that Angel will come here, come to find me. He's not finished with me. I know that for sure."

Ellie thought she'd figured out why Sue was so determined to tell about Angel.

"What you're saying is that you're afraid you've involved me with your brother by living here on my land. If he comes for you, I might be affected."

"That's right, and I'm sorry. I wanted to tell you when Lane took the job, but I was afraid you wouldn't hire him.

We needed to get away from where we were, and I didn't want to do anything to hurt our chances."

"It wouldn't have made any difference," Ellie said. "I hired Lane because he was the right man for the job and because I liked you and Laurie. No story about your brother would have changed my mind, no matter how bad he is."

"You haven't heard it all yet," Sue said. "Angel ran away and left our mother and me there in that burning house. I tried to get her out, but I couldn't. I pulled and pulled on her, but I couldn't move her. She was unconscious, and I couldn't use my right arm. I stayed as long as I could, until my hair was starting to singe. But finally I had to decide whether to leave my mother or die."

Sue looked down at the table. "I left."

Ellie reached out to touch her hand. "No one could blame you for that."

Sue swallowed hard and said, "You'd be surprised. My father blamed me. After my mother's funeral, he sent me to live with an aunt in San Antonio, and I never saw him again."

"You saw Angel again, though."

Sue looked up. "How did you know?"

"It was just a feeling."

"Well, you're right. I saw Angel again. Oh, yes, I saw him. Whenever he got in trouble, and he got in trouble all the time, he'd come back to his family. It was his idea that the family had to help him because that's what families were for, and some of the time he did get help. I don't think my father ever did anything for him, but he turned up in San Antonio more than once. And every time my aunt would give him money or food or a place to hide out for a while. Whatever he needed."

"Had you told your aunt what happened that night at your house?"

"I'd told her, and I'm sorry I did. That's why she helped Angel. She was afraid of him. But I didn't blame her for that. So was I."

"He didn't try to hurt you again?"

"I stayed away from him, and I don't think I slept a wink whenever he came to my aunt's house. You should have seen the way he looked at me, smiling that angel smile of his. If you didn't know him, you'd think he was just back from choir practice or maybe come home from church where he'd recited scripture for the congregation. But I knew him better than that. I knew what he was thinking."

"You're safe here, though," Ellie said. "There's no reason for him to come after you here."

"Oh, yes, there is," Sue said. "That's why I have the dreams."

Chapter 8

Ben Jephson knew he was in deep trouble. He was in with a bunch of killers, and he'd more or less helped them kill three men. Four if you counted Yankee Tom, though maybe the law would let them off for that one. But Jephson wasn't a killer, not really. In his whole life, he'd never wanted to hurt anyone. He just kept winding up in the wrong place at the wrong time.

The plain fact of the matter was that of all the men behind the walls in Huntsville, at least ninety-nine percent of them claimed they were innocent. And they were all lying.

Jephson, on the other hand, had never claimed anything, though he was actually innocent of any wrongdoing. Or at least any intentional wrongdoing. Or at least of killing anyone, which is what he'd been accused of.

He'd been out of a job and on the prod when he'd fallen in with two men who offered him some coffee and a meal late one evening. He'd still been with the two when the posse caught up with them.

How was Jephson to know that they'd robbed a bank, killed a teller, and then wounded three other men in their getaway?

One of the men, by the name of Shepard, was both quicker and meaner than Jephson would have guessed. When he realized what was going to happen, he whipped out his pistol, shot his partner, and then shot Jephson. The bullet slapped off Jephson's hat and plowed a furrow along the right side of his head. He hardly had the time to blink before he was lying on the ground, unconscious.

When the posse arrived, Shepard said, "I fell in with these two drifters last night, and it just dawned on me who they was. When I mentioned that bank holdup to 'em, they drew on me, but I got in the first licks."

The posse members believed him, either because it was convenient for them to do so or because Shepard was a convincing liar, not that it made much difference to Jephson or the partner either way.

Jephson lived, the partner didn't. Shepard even collected a small reward and no doubt the thanks of the grateful townspeople, who were grateful that their bank got most of its money back.

When Jephson came to, no one was interested in hearing his side of the story, and there was no one about to back him up, Shepard having lit a shuck for parts unknown with his reward and with the little part of the bank's money that he'd managed to hold on to.

The jury that was convened had no sympathy for Jephson, who counted himself lucky that they hadn't sen-

tenced him to hang, which they would have done if any of
the prosecution's witnesses had been able to swear he was
one of the two who'd robbed the bank, which they couldn't,
not because he hadn't been there but because Shepard
and his partner had covered the lower halves of their
faces.

As it was, Jephson got life in prison, and his life
probably wouldn't have lasted very long if his reputation
hadn't preceded him. By the time he was locked up, everyone behind the walls knew he was a robber and a man-
killer, and they didn't try to mess with him.

His appearance helped, too. He knew that he looked
mean as a snake, even if he wasn't. The other prisoners
wouldn't bother him as long as they were afraid of him, so
he kept his mouth shut, tried to look meaner than he was,
and went about his business. And although he knew he
was never going to get out of prison, at least he was alive,
and that was just about the best he could hope for.

Or so he'd thought. Now he was free again. The storm
had passed, there was a big blue sky over his head, and he
could see a couple of buzzards spinning lazily in the distance. For a second or two he could almost imagine that
the last three years behind prison walls had just been a
bad dream.

But he knew that wasn't true. He was free, but he was
mixed up with killers a lot worse than those two bank robbers, and he'd already been a party to something far worse
than the robbers had ever thought about.

He knew he had two choices: stick with Angel or

strike out on his own. He didn't like either option. If he went out on his own, he was bound to get caught. He didn't have any weapons, any money, or any clothes.

Angel had the sawed-off shotgun, and he'd stripped Rankin's clothes off and taken them, though they didn't fit him very well. There hadn't been any need for them to bother with Bowman. His clothes wouldn't have come close to fitting any of them. He'd had a couple of dollars in his pockets, but Angel had taken those. No one had complained.

Now they were making their way somewhere, but Jephson wasn't at all sure just where. Maybe they were just drifting.

Angel had said something about wanting to visit his family, but Jephson thought he might be joking about that. Angel didn't give a damn about anybody or anything. It was hard to believe he even had a family.

Hoot Riley wanted to find a farmhouse and kill whoever was in it and take whatever was there. Angel seemed to think it was a good idea. They needed more clothes and some guns.

Abilene Jack didn't appear to care much what they did as long as they got something to eat before dark.

"They'll know at the prison that something's gone wrong by now, and they'll be out after us," he said. "We need to find us a place to hole up for the night and maybe get a little rest. And I'd surely like something to eat before it gets too much later. My belly think's my throat's been cut."

Angel laughed. "It's not like you're used to eatin' the best of food. You wouldn't know what to do with a biscuit if it didn't have wigglers in it."

Jephson thought of the food he'd been eating for the last three years or so, if you could call it food. When you got meat, it was spoiled. And Angel was right about the biscuits. They were always full of weevils.

"Find us that farmhouse, we'll find something good to eat," Hoot said. "*Real* biscuits, and maybe some honey to go with 'em. Maybe find us a woman, too." He smacked his lips.

Jephson knew what Hoot was thinking, all right, and it didn't just have to do with food. Jephson could even understand it in a way. They'd been locked up for a long time, after all. But to Jephson's way of thinking, Hoot was a little on the crazy side. If Hoot had his way, every lawman in the state would be on their trail.

"We're all dead men anyhow," Hoot said, as if reading Jephson's thoughts. "They'll hunt us from hell to breakfast for killing Bowman and Rankin. We might as well have us a little fun while we got the chance."

Hoot was already having more fun than Jephson, because Hoot was getting to ride. So was Angel. Jack and Jephson were walking, which wasn't exactly easy in the mud that the storm had created. It was warming up, and the walking was hard. But Jephson wasn't complaining. He hadn't been astraddle a horse or a mule in four years. He knew that Hoot was going to pay a price when he got off that mule.

"We're not here to have fun," Angel said. "I've got some business to finish with my family, and if you're goin' with me, you'll have to wait to have your fun. We don't need to be slowing down for any shenanigans."

"We could use some grub, though," Jack said. "I don't know where your family is, but if they ain't within another hour or so's walkin', I'd just as soon find us something to eat."

Jephson agreed with the sentiment, though he knew they weren't going to be able to walk into a town, find a café, and order up some steak and gravy.

Hoot agreed, too. "There's bound to be a farm along in here somewhere. There's little farms all over this part of the country. And like I said, find that farmhouse, and we'll find us some food."

Angel didn't comment.

"What kind of business you got with your family, anyway?" Hoot asked. "I don't see why you're so het up to see them all of a sudden. I don't remember you gettin' any letters from them while we were locked up, and they damn sure didn't pay you any calls. I bet they don't want to see you anywhere near as much as you want to see them."

Angel smiled in a way that made Jephson's stomach feel queasy, the way it felt when he ate that prison meat. Suddenly he wasn't very hungry after all.

"That's one bet you'd surely win," Angel said.

Chapter 9

—⟡—

"We turned Angel in," Sue Tolbert said, looking down at the steaming coffee in the mug that sat on the table in front of her. "Lane and I did. I didn't even think he knew where we were living, and he didn't think I knew what he'd done. But he found us somehow, and I'd already heard about the man he killed."

Ellie took a sip of her own coffee. She liked to drink it while it was so hot that it nearly scalded her tongue, even though she could barely taste it. Then she said, "How did you hear?"

Sue turned the thick coffee mug in her hands. "Lane has a brother, too, but he's not like Angel. Just the opposite, I guess you could say. His name's Brady, and he's a Texas Ranger. He figured that Angel might show up at our house sooner or later. He sent a telegram to tell us that Angel had killed a man in a fight in San Antonio. The man was unarmed. Angel had stabbed him ten times."

"He couldn't very well claim self-defense, then, could he," Ellie said.

Sue smiled ruefully. "If you believe that, you don't know Angel very well. I don't think he ever took responsibility for a single thing he did. It was always someone else's fault, never his."

Ellie nodded. She'd known people like that.

"I'm sure the man in San Antonio wasn't the first that Angel had killed," Sue said. "But this was the first time that there were witnesses."

"You can't be sure about any other times," Ellie said. "Maybe he's not as bad as you think."

"No, I can't be sure." Sue sipped her coffee, then set the mug back on the table. "But he's as bad as I think. He's probably even worse. I've heard plenty of stories about things he's supposed to have done, and I'm sure most of them are true, even though I don't have any proof."

Ellie understood what Sue meant. There were some things that you just knew, even if you didn't have any evidence to back them up.

"Anyway," Sue said, "Angel turned up, just like Brady thought he would. When I told Angel I knew what had happened, he said that he'd been pushed into the fight and that the man had pulled a pistol on him. He asked if he could stay with us for a few days, but I knew he meant a few weeks. He always stayed that long when he turned up. They wouldn't give up the hunt for him in just a few days. So I didn't give him any argument. I told him he could stay, and then that night I told Lane to go into town the next day and send a telegram to Brady to let him know where Angel was."

"Didn't Angel suspect anything?"

"No. We never let on that there was anything for him to worry about, and he was used to getting his way with us. He probably never dreamed that we'd turn him over to the law."

"What abut Laurie?" Ellie wanted to know.

"That's a funny thing," Sue said, but she wasn't smiling. "For some reason, Laurie always seemed to like Angel. I could never figure out why."

The thought of Laurie associating with someone like Angel gave Ellie a chill.

"Was there trouble when the Rangers came?" she asked.

"There was only one Ranger, and that was Brady. They wouldn't bother to send two for just one man, not even a man like Angel."

Sue sipped her coffee. There was a distant look in her eyes, as if she were seeing her brother again. When she set the mug back on the table, she said, "There wasn't any trouble, not really. Angel wasn't expecting anyone to come for him. Brady took him pretty much by surprise."

"I guess Angel wasn't too happy about that," Ellie said.

Sue drank the rest of her coffee and set the mug on the table. She looked down into the mug as if she might be trying to read the future there. Then she looked up at Ellie.

"Happy?" she said. "No, he wasn't happy. He said that someday he was going to come back and that we'd all be sorry for what we'd done to him."

"So it was all your fault," Ellie said.

"That's right. He was the one who'd killed a man, but we were to blame for him being arrested. That's the way Angel always sees things."

"And you said he has a long memory for things like that."

"Oh, he does. I wasn't exaggerating about that."

"Well, then," Ellie said, "I'm not surprised you have bad dreams about him. But if you turned him in, you don't have to worry. They put him in jail, didn't they?"

Sue nodded. "Oh, yes. They put him in the prison at Huntsville."

"That's where he belongs," Ellie said. "He won't be getting out of there for a long time."

"I guess you're right," Sue said. "And it's easy to think that way in the daytime. But sometimes at night, I start to worry. One of those stories I heard about Angel said that he killed two men up in Tascosa because they cheated him in a card game."

Ellie thought that anyone who got into a card game in Tascosa should have known he was going to get cheated, but she didn't say so.

"They put him in jail that time, too," Sue went on. "Not in Huntsville, but in Abilene. Or that's the way the story went. He was in about a week before he escaped, and then one night he shot both the men who'd supposedly cheated him. In the back."

"So he's a coward, then," Ellie said.

"Oh, no. He's no coward. He most likely shot them in

the back because it was just more convenient for him that way. I'm sure he would have enjoyed watching their eyes when he had the drop on them and they knew what was about to happen."

Ellie thought that was a terrible thing to say about anyone, much less your own brother. She hoped she never met Angel.

When she said as much to Sue, the other woman rubbed her hand over her face. Then she said, "I hope you never meet him, either. There's not an ounce of good in him that I know of."

Ellie stood up from the table and smiled. It wasn't a very nice smile, but it was the best she could do.

"I think I've heard enough about your brother," she said. "Why don't we go in and see what Laurie's doing."

"Laurie," Sue said. "You know, I was afraid to have a child at one time. I was afraid that if I did, it might turn out to be like Angel."

Ellie picked up the coffee mugs. "Laurie looks like an angel, for sure. You just go on in there with her, and I'll take these mugs to Juana. And don't you worry about your brother. He won't be bothering you here."

Sue shivered as if a cold draft had blown through the room.

"I'm sure you're right," she said, but she didn't look sure at all.

Chapter 10

Hoot Riley looked at the little farmhouse that stood off in the distance. It was about a half hour after dark, and there was lamplight flickering in the windows of the house. Hoot had no idea how many people were inside, but that didn't bother him in the least.

"There's our supper," he said.

Jephson slapped at a mosquito that was buzzing around his head. "It'd be takin' a big chance for us just to walk up there and ask for a handout."

"We're not all goin'," Angel said. "Just one of us."

"Which one?" Jephson asked.

Angel inclined his head toward Riley. "Hoot. He looks like a farm boy."

"What about his clothes?" Abilene Jack asked. "You don't see many farm boys wearing prison duds."

"He'll be standin' in the dark. Nobody'll notice what he's wearin' till it's way too late."

"There'll be a dog," Jephson said. "There's always a dog or two around a place like that."

"I don't care about any damn dog," Hoot said. "He prob'ly smells the mules already. What's he gonna do, bark at me and let 'em know I'm comin'? He's gonna bark at the mules anyhow, and I don't give a damn if they know I'm comin'."

"He's right," Angel said. "It won't make any difference to them."

Hoot grinned and wiped the back of his hand across his dry mouth. "You gonna let me have the shotgun?"

"That's right," Angel said. "We'll be waitin' out here in the trees till you do what has to be done."

"What if there's too many of 'em in there?" Jephson asked.

"Goddammit to hell, you worry too much, Jephson," Hoot told him. "You act like there's gonna be a troop of soldiers layin' in wait for us, but you don't have to worry about it. I know all about farms like that. There won't be nobody inside that house except some old man and his wife, and they won't put up any kind of a fight."

To tell the truth, Hoot wouldn't have minded a little fight. He didn't see much sport in killing some old coot and his wife. Maybe there'd be a young couple in there. Maybe he wouldn't kill the wife until she'd showed him a good time.

Angel handed him the shotgun and a couple of extra shells.

"Whoever's in there," he said, "don't waste any time with them."

* * *

When Brady Tolbert arrived at the big adobe building that served as Texas Ranger headquarters in Del Rio, he saw Northrup and Cody under a shade tree. They were playing checkers on a board set up on an upturned water barrel.

Northrup was a stocky young man in his early twenties. Cody was older and more experienced, one of the best Rangers that Brady had met. Like Brady, he was tall, lean, and toughened by long nights in the saddle and long days under the hot Texas sun.

"Afternoon, Tolbert," Cody said when Brady had tied his horse to the hitch rail. "You got a meeting with the Old Man?"

Brady nodded. "He sent for me, all right. Any idea of what's going on?"

"Not unless you count me winnin' six games in a row from young Northrup here. If you had to win a checker game to get in the Rangers, he'd still be walkin' behind a mule back on his daddy's farm."

"I almost got you that last time," Northrup said. "You ambushed me with that triple jump."

Cody grinned. "You got to watch out for ambushes, boy. You too, Brady. No tellin' what the Old Man's got in mind for you today."

Brady agreed and went on into the headquarters building. A Ranger named Seth, even younger than Northrup, sat at the desk just inside the door.

"Hey, Brady," he said. "The captain wants to see you right away."

"So I heard," Brady said, walking past the desk. He tapped on the door of the Ranger captain's office and went inside without waiting for an invitation.

The captain stood up when Brady entered. He was a ramrod-straight man who dressed all in black except for the white shirt he habitually wore with his black string tie. He looked more like a hellfire-and-brimstone preacher than a Ranger, and in fact he had been a preacher at one time in his life.

"Good afternoon, Captain," Brady said. "You got something for me today?"

"That I have," the captain said. "Have a seat, and I'll tell you all about it."

Brady sat in a hard straight-backed chair, and the captain settled himself behind his desk. He picked up a piece of paper and glanced down at it.

"I have a telegram here that might interest you," he said.

Brady didn't like the sound of that. In his experience, telegrams never brought good news.

This one was no exception.

"It's about someone you know," the captain said. "I'm sure you remember Angel Ware."

Angel Ware, Brady thought. *Mean as a rattler and twice as dangerous*.

"I remember him," he told the captain. "He's in the prison up in Huntsville, where I put him."

"Not anymore," the captain said. "He's escaped, him and three others. Ben Jephson, Abilene Jack Sturdivant, and a youngster named Hoot Riley. Killed a couple of guards and two trusties."

Brady wasn't surprised to hear it. Three of the names weren't familiar to him, but Angel Ware wasn't the kind to stay behind bars if any chance to escape presented itself.

"That's not all," the captain said. "Last night, Ware and the other three went into a farmhouse and killed two people, the owner and his wife. Used the guard's shotgun on 'em, then took their food and an old pistol that the man had. They've probably picked up more weapons by now."

"You think Angel's the leader?" Brady asked.

" 'Course he is. Those other three? They're bad. Killers, every one of 'em. But they're Sunday school teachers compared to Angel Ware."

"You think they'll stick together?"

"I'd bet on it. There's something about a man like Ware that draws others to him if they're of like mind."

"So I guess I should ask what you want me to do about it," Brady said. "Is Ware heading this way?"

The captain looked grim. "I don't know. I thought maybe you could tell me."

"I don't have any idea where he's going," Brady said. "He's crazy, though, I can tell you that. He might go anywhere."

"I thought he might be going back where he went the last time," the captain said.

Brady thought about it. "You could be right, except that he won't find his sister there. She's moved away."

"That was a wise idea. Do you think Ware can find her?"

Brady shrugged. "Hard to say. Texas is a big place."

"But you can find her, can't you?"

"She's married to my brother, if that's what you mean."

"You'd better go there, then. It wouldn't hurt to put a watch on her, just in case Angel shows up."

Brady stood up. "All right. She's living up in Blanco these days, with my brother and their daughter."

"Blanco? Wasn't there some trouble there a year or so back?"

The captain looked down at the telegram he was still holding, as if the answer to his question might be there.

"I remember now," he said, looking back at Brady. "The bank was robbed, and a couple of men were killed. We sent a Ranger up there, but by the time he arrived, two of the robbers were dead, killed by the woman whose husband they'd murdered. The other robber had the money, I'm sorry to say. He got clean away. He's probably in Mexico, and he'll stay there if he's smart."

"The woman's name is Ellie Taine," Brady said. "She has a ranch just out of Blanco. My brother's her foreman. Do you want me to head up that way today?"

"Right this minute wouldn't be too soon," the captain said. "You brought Ware in the last time without firing a shot. I don't think you'll be quite so lucky this time, should you meet up with him again."

For some reason, Brady didn't think so either. "We'll see," he said.

Chapter 11

— ❧❦❧ —

Angel felt good with a knife in his boot again, even if the knife wasn't a very good one and the boots didn't fit him right. He knew that he'd get a better knife sooner or later, and Rankin's boots, if a little too big, were better than what Angel had been wearing for the last couple of years.

He also felt better after eating. They hadn't taken the time to do that at the farmhouse, but after they'd stopped, they'd had some canned tomatoes and beans they'd brought away with them. It wasn't much, but it was filling enough for the time being.

Angel looked over at Abilene Jack, who was now dressed in a work shirt and some patched denim pants that they'd taken from the farmhouse. The clothes fit Jack about the way the boots fit Angel, but they'd do.

Jack was talking to Jephson, who was also wearing some of the dead farmer's clothes, as was Hoot Riley, who was sleeping in the shade of a yaupon bush with his head on a saddle. Three pairs of pants and three shirts were about all the clothes the farmer owned, and not a one of the men was exactly the farmer's size. It didn't matter, though. They'd needed the clothes, and the fit was close enough.

They were a motley-looking bunch, Angel thought, but at least they didn't look quite so much like escaped prisoners. They didn't look like the town mayor, either, but then they weren't going to be running for the legislature or trying to borrow money at a bank. So they didn't exactly need churchgoers' clothes.

Angel stood up and walked over to Jack. "Did you feed the mules?"

There were four mules now. They'd taken a couple that had until recently belonged to the farmer. They'd taken several bags of grain, too, along with the saddle that Hoot was using for a pillow.

"I fed 'em," Jack said. "They're ready to go whenever we are."

Angel wasn't quite as ready as the mules to be on his way, however. They had made camp by a little creek that was well-shaded by tall pine and elm trees and well away from any main trails. There was hardly a breath of wind, and the creek was almost perfectly still. Now and then a leaf from an elm tree would float down and land on the muddy brown surface of the water.

"We'll stay here until dark," Angel said. "Then we'll be moving along. Better if we travel at night from now on. You two might want to get some rest."

Jack shot Jephson a glance. "Me and Ben have been talkin'," he said.

Angel squatted down beside them. "I could see that. What's on your minds?"

Jack ducked his head as if he didn't want to meet Angel's steady blue gaze.

"Well, we've sorta been wondering about this family visit of yours. Not that it's any of our business, but—"

"You're right," Angel said, cutting him off. "It's not any of your business." He smiled, though the smile didn't touch his icy eyes. "But if you're going along with me, I'll tell you about it."

"I guess we'll be goin' along," Jephson said. "That's what we've been talkin' about, tryin' to make up our minds."

"You can go with me or take off on your own," Angel said. He didn't much care one way or the other. "Up to you."

"It's not that we don't think you know what you're doin'," Jack said. "It's just that . . ."

Jack's voice trailed off, but Jephson finished the sentence for him. "It's just that we don't like what Hoot did last night."

Angel relaxed and settled back against the trunk of an elm tree. "You afraid of a little killin'?"

Jack shook his head. "That ain't it. It's just that it don't seem too smart to be callin' attention to ourselves that way."

"Those people had something we needed," Angel said. "They weren't gonna give it to us just because we asked pretty-like. So we took it the easiest way we could."

Jephson said, "Yeah, it was easy. But it let every lawman in Texas know where we were."

Angel laughed. "You think they didn't know already? Those mules and us left a trail in that mud that even a Hob Bowman could've followed with his eyes shut."

Jack and Jephson evidently hadn't thought of that. They looked around them with jerky movements of their heads as if they were expecting some badge carrier to step out from behind a pine tree and arrest them on the spot.

Angel watched them for a couple of seconds, then said, "We covered up a lot better after we left the farmhouse. The ground was a good bit harder in places, so our tracks wouldn't be so easy to find. And after we got into these piney woods it wasn't so muddy."

The pine trees stretched for miles, and Angel had headed for them as soon as they'd left the farmhouse. It wasn't going to be easy for anyone to track them in the woods.

"Besides, we had a good start on any posse they get up," he said. "They couldn't have got after us until they found Bowman and Rankin. Then they'd have to get some men together. Prob'ly didn't get started till this mornin', if then. They might not be started yet."

Jack looked down at the creek where a snapping turtle was showing its mouth above the water.

"You're sayin' we shouldn't worry, then?"

"Worry if you want to. Don't matter to me."

"If we keep on killin' farmers, we'll be cuttin' such a wide swath that they'll catch up to us soon enough," Jephson said.

"We don't have to kill anybody else," Angel said. "We got enough now to get where I want to go."

Jephson nodded over to where Hoot was still sleeping peacefully under the yaupon.

"What about him?"

"What do you mean?"

"Hoot's not gonna want to stop killin'," Jephson said. "I think he kinda likes it."

Angel thought about the previous night. Hoot had knocked on the door of the farmhouse and shot the farmer as soon as the door opened. Then Hoot had stepped inside and fired the shotgun again. He'd still been smiling when Angel and the others got there.

"You could be right," Angel told Jephson, with a smile of his own. "But there won't be any chance for him to kill anybody else. I don't want us to be callin' attention to ourselves until we get where we're headed."

"What's in it for us if we stick with you?" Abilene Jack asked.

"Not a damned thing," Angel said. "Tell you the truth, it might be better if we split up. It'd give the law more trails to follow."

"What if they caught up with one of us, and that one told where you were goin'?" Jephson wanted to know.

"Well, now," Angel said. "That wouldn't make me any too happy. It'd sure be bad for the fella that did that if he and I ever wound up in the same jail again."

Jephson shifted uncomfortably. "Nobody's gonna tell

where you're goin'. Hell, we don't even know. What's this about your family, anyhow? You said you'd tell us."

Jephson knew that for the time being Angel was his best hope for staying out of prison, but he didn't like the idea of committing to him without knowing the whole story. At the same time, he didn't want to make Angel mad. He decided it might be best to appear ready to fall in with Angel's plans and then, if he had to, try to break away later on. So he said, "It's just that I'd feel a little better if I knew what I was gettin' into."

Angel glanced at the snapping turtle in the creek. Some people didn't like those turtles, but Angel did. Folks said that if you let them clamp down on a tree limb thick enough that they couldn't bite through it, they'd never let it go. Or at least they wouldn't let go till it thundered. In Texas that could be a long time. The turtles reminded Angel of himself that way.

"Let's just say that my sister and I have a little unfinished business," he told Jephson. "You know how families are."

"What kind of business?" Jack asked.

"Personal business," Angel said. "It won't have anything to do with you."

"Gonna be any killin'?"

"Well, now, that's a good question. Right now, I don't think so. It's just not what I have in mind. But you never know how these things are gonna work out."

Angel knew that Jack probably wouldn't believe him, but he was telling the truth. He'd waited more than two years to get back at Hob Bowman, but he hadn't known exactly what he would do. He'd just known he would do something. The same thing held for his sister and her husband. They were going to pay for sending him to prison, but he hadn't decided how. First he'd find them. Then he'd see how things stood.

"You ain't makin' things very clear," Abilene Jack said. "I don't see how we can make up our minds on what to do from that."

Angel stood up. "Too bad. It's the best I can do. I don't have any plan. I'll just have to see how things work out and then make up my mind. If that's not good enough for you, you can take off on your own. I'll let you have one of the mules."

"That's mighty generous of you," Jephson said dryly.

Angel was beginning to wonder about Jephson. Seemed like he was a little leery. Not the best kind of man to have with you if things got rough. And Abilene Jack wasn't turning out to be much better.

"It is generous of me, ain't it," he said. "You two think things over a little longer. You don't have to make your minds up right now. But you'd better decide before it gets good dark. We'll be leavin' about then."

"We'll let you know," Abilene Jack said.

Chapter 12

—◆—⇥⇤—◆—

Brady Tolbert thought he had one advantage on Angel Ware. For all Angel knew, Sue and Lane were still living up around Fort Worth instead of just outside Blanco. The captain had sent a request for a Ranger to be on the lookout for Angel in Fort Worth, and if they were lucky, Angel would be caught there and never get to Blanco.

Even if Angel evaded the Ranger and managed to find out where Sue was living, Brady would have a good head start on him, so Brady hoped to get to Sue a long time before Angel did.

It might have worked out that way, too, if Brady's horse hadn't stepped in a hole about a day and a half out of Del Rio.

Brady felt it was at least partly his own fault. He'd been thinking about the job he was to do and not paying enough attention to where his big lineback dun was stepping, but then he told himself that the horse should have been paying attention, too.

Some armadillo had rooted out a hole, or maybe the

ground had just washed that way in the recent rains that had passed through. It didn't make any difference. Brady had to go back to Del Rio, leading his horse and losing another three days in the process. By the time he got on his way again, Angel would have had plenty of time to learn that his sister was no longer living where she had been that last time he'd seen her.

But maybe Angel hadn't been able to learn where she'd gone. Brady hoped not. It was nearly all he thought about as he made the best time he could toward Blanco.

Angel felt perfectly at home in the Salty Dog Saloon in the section of Fort Worth known as Hell's Half Acre.

The sun was hot and bright in the street, and if Angel took a deep breath, he could smell the stockyards. But inside the saloon it was cool and quiet, and all he could smell were cheap whiskey, the sawdust on the floor, and the stale perfume of the saloon girls that lingered in the air from the previous night.

The Salty Dog wasn't crowded; it was the middle of the afternoon, and at that time of day only the serious drinkers were there. Angel and Hoot were sitting at a table well in the back with a man named Kincaid, who had only three fingers on his left hand and a patch where his right eye had once been.

Angel wasn't too happy with Kincaid.

"I don't quite understand what you're tryin' to tell me," Angel said.

Kincaid didn't mind that Angel was upset. After all, Kincaid had a drink in his good hand, and that was all he cared about. Within the last few years, he had turned into a man to whom only two times in the day really mattered: the times when he had a drink and the times he didn't. Taking it all in all, he much preferred the times when he did.

He tried to sit up straighter in his chair, failed, and allowed himself to slump. Then he took a hefty swallow of whiskey, wiped the back of his hand across his mouth, and said, "I'm tryin' to tell you that nobody knows where your sister's gone, that's what I'm tryin' to tell you. What's so hard to understand about that?"

"That's not what I paid you to find out," Angel said.

Kincaid tried to smile, but it didn't come off very well. Probably it was the look in Angel's pale eyes that discouraged him.

"You didn't pay me much," he whined.

"Want me to take him out back?" Hoot asked. "See if I can get our money back?"

Angel grinned. Hoot was acting as if he'd worked for weeks for the money they'd paid Kincaid, but the truth was they'd stolen it from some drunken cowboys a couple of nights earlier in the week.

"I don't want the money back," Angel said. "I want to know where my sister's gone."

Kincaid said, "I wish I could help you, I truly do. But far's I can tell she didn't leave word with nobody where she was headed. She and that husband of hers just packed up, took that little gal of theirs, and lit out one day."

"Little gal?" Hoot said, looking at Angel. "You didn't say nothin' about a little gal."

"Purty little thing, they tell me," Kincaid said.

Hoot smiled. "Well, well."

"Never mind about that," Angel said. "I think Mr. Kincaid knows more than he's tellin' us."

Kincaid set his empty whiskey glass on the table. His hand was shaking, and the glass tapped the table twice.

"Wh-what makes you say a thing like that?" he asked Angel.

"Because you talk too much. I wonder why that is. Maybe you don't think I paid you enough. It looks to me like you messed around and found out things I didn't ask you about."

Kincaid tried to stand up, but Hoot reached out and put a hand on his shoulder, shoving him back into his chair.

"Now I have to tell you something," Angel said. "I paid you once, and there's no use you tryin' to get any more out of me by sellin' extra information. It just don't work that way."

"Tell him how it *does* work," Hoot said, his hand still resting on Kincaid's shoulder.

Angel's right hand was a blur as it dipped to his boot top and came out with the Bowie knife he'd stolen to replace the inferior model he'd taken from the farmer. Before Kincaid could jerk out of the way, the tip of the blade was an inch from his single eyeball.

Kincaid kicked his boots against the floor in an

attempt to move his chair backward, but his heels slipped in the sawdust. Hoot jumped up to stand behind him and grabbed his head in both hands, holding it firmly in place.

Angel leaned across the table until his face was almost touching Kincaid's. He braced his elbow on the table and held the knife steady.

"Here's how it works," Angel told Kincaid. "I can blind you before you can wink. I can pop that eyeball like a grape."

"I ain't winkin'," Kincaid said.

Angel looked around the saloon. No one was paying them any attention. This was what passed for a quiet afternoon in Hell's Half Acre.

The bartender was studiously looking the other way and wiping the top of the bar hard enough to take the shine off it. The few other customers were looking at their drinks. The only woman in sight was sleeping in a chair, her head resting on a tabletop, her mouth open.

Angel moved the knife a fraction closer to Kincaid's watery brown eye.

"No, you ain't winkin', but you ain't been tellin' us the entire truth, either."

Kincaid was having trouble breathing. "Yes, I am. I wouldn't lie to a fella like you."

"I think you would, but I guess I'm gonna have to put out that eye to make you admit it."

"Let me do it," Hoot said. "Just one little shove and that eyeball will turn to jelly."

"Jesus!" Kincaid said. "I swear I don't know where

that woman is. I might be able to point you at someone who does know, but I don't. I swear it!"

Angel relaxed slightly and moved the knife to a safer distance from Kincaid's eye. Two inches or so.

"All right, then, tell me what you know. I might decide to let you keep on seein'."

Kincaid was sweating heavily. "I asked around the place where she used to stay, like you told me to. The old man who bought it wouldn't tell me a thing, but I got a feelin' that his wife would've told if he'd given her the chance. She's the one mentioned the little gal. Soon's she did, the old man sent her off out of the room. That's it. That's all I know. I thought it might be worth a little somethin' extra if I told you about the woman."

"It is," Angel said. "It's worth your eye."

As fast as it had appeared, the knife was gone, back in its hiding place. Angel leaned back in his chair, and Hoot released his grip on Kincaid's head. Kincaid slumped forward and caught himself on the table.

"You could've saved yourself a lot of trouble by telling us to start with," Angel said.

"I didn't know you were crazy then," Kincaid said. "I know it now."

"It's a good thing to keep in mind," Angel told him. He looked at Hoot. "Let's go."

They left the saloon without looking back. Kincaid stayed in his chair, slumped forward so that his chin was resting on the table. He looked at the empty whiskey glass and wished he had the strength to order another drink.

Chapter 13

⊶ ══╬══ ⊷

"I think his family's got somethin' he wants," Abilene Jack said. "How 'bout you?"

"Makes sense," Jephson agreed.

He couldn't see any other reason why Angel was so eager to find his sister. As far as Jephson knew, there was no affection between the two. Angel had never mentioned his family to Jephson, or to anyone else in prison as far as Jephson knew.

"Maybe it's money," Jack said. "I'll bet it's money. Maybe he'll share it out with us."

"Maybe," Jephson said, not really believing it. Angel didn't seem like the sharing type to him.

Jephson and Abilene Jack were in the room they'd rented in a cheap hotel not far from the Salty Dog. Every chance he had, Jephson had been talking to Jack about splitting off from Angel and Hoot, but Jack wasn't having any of it.

"I think we oughta stick with him for a while longer,"

Jack said. "He's kept us in pocket money so far, and we ain't had any run-ins with the law."

Jephson pointed out that they couldn't keep robbing drunk cowboys in dark alleys forever. Sooner or later they were going to get caught, even in Fort Worth.

"Angel's got a plan," Jack said, and proceeded to explain what he thought the plan was. "He's gonna find out where his family is, and then we'll go there. We'll get whatever it is that he wants, and then we'll get out of the state. Maybe head down to Mexico. The law won't bother us down there. We can live like kings down there."

If that was the plan, Jephson thought, it really didn't sound too bad, especially the part about living like kings. But Jephson wasn't sure that was the plan at all. Angel had never spelled it out like that. He'd just let Jack draw his own conclusions, and Jephson wasn't sure the conclusions were correct.

"What if it's somethin' else?" he said.

Jack didn't seem worried by the prospect. "If it is, Angel will let us know. He's just bein' careful now. He don't want any of us to wind up back in Huntsville."

Jephson didn't want to wind up back in Huntsville either, but was Angel really being careful? That was another thing Jephson worried about. Sure, Angel had hired somebody to go around asking questions about his family instead of doing it himself. You could call that careful if you had a mind to, Jephson supposed.

But how careful was it to have anyone at all asking

questions? And why had Angel's family left the area? Seemed to Jephson that they were doing all they could to keep Angel from finding them again.

Not that Jephson blamed them.

Still, as far as he could tell after considering everything he could think of, Jephson figured he was just as well off sticking with Angel as he would be in going off on his own. Not being a real outlaw himself, Jephson was sure he'd probably do something stupid and get caught the first day. Jack was a little smarter about things, and Jephson figured the two of them could strike out on their own and maybe stay out of prison without Angel's help. But Jack just didn't seem interested.

"I guess you're right," Jephson told Jack. "I don't want to go back behind those walls, and maybe Angel's the man who can keep us out."

What Jephson might have said was that he was scared. He was scared of Angel, and he was scared of Hoot. But he knew he couldn't tell Jack that. Besides, he was more scared of getting caught and sent back to Huntsville than he was of Angel or Hoot. He just didn't know what to do.

"If anybody can keep us out of that prison," Jack said, "it's Angel."

Jephson wished he believed him.

Hoot rode his mule right up to the house. He hated to admit it, but he'd gotten almost fond of the critter. Abilene

Jack had been right; a mule was in some ways better than a horse, and this one hadn't tried to bite Hoot a single time. It had tried to kick him once, but Hoot figured that was his own fault. He should've known better than to give it a chance. It wouldn't happen again.

Hoot slid off the mule's back with a country-boy grin plastered on his freckled face. He looked like he'd just come into town from some farm twenty miles away from anywhere and needed a job to help him get started on his own.

He walked up to the front door with his hat crushed in his hand. The yard was well kept, and there was a little flower bed with some petunias in it.

Hoot hated the place. People who lived in houses like that were the kind of people who'd always given him trouble: Sunday school teachers, preachers, lawmen. He resisted the urge to kick the blooms off the petunias and knocked on the door.

The knock was answered by a big woman in a cotton dress. She looked nothing at all like a Sunday school teacher. Her face was weathered and red as if she worked outside a lot, and her hair was done up in a bun on the back of her head.

"Well?" she said, looking Hoot over with something less than approval.

Hoot gave her his country-boy grin. "Howdy, ma'am. I heard you could use some help around this place, and I'm just the fella that can give it to you. I'm mighty handy with one thing and another. I can chop wood, patch your roof, just about any little job you might need done."

The woman didn't return Hoot's smile. "Somebody told you wrong. We don't need any help around here. My husband and I can keep up our own place."

Hoot scratched his head, puzzled. "You ain't Miz Tolbert?"

"I'm Miz Wallace. The Tolberts haven't lived here in more than a year."

"I'll swear," Hoot said, looking abashed. "I guess somebody was funnin' me. People are always doin' that kind of thing. I guess I look simple or something." He gave the woman what he hoped was an appealing smile. "I don't suppose you know what happened to the Tolberts, do you? I surely could use a job."

"I heard they moved to a little town called Blanco. I imagine that's a little too far for you to go looking for a job."

Hoot settled his hat back on his head. "You never can tell about a thing like that," he said.

Chapter 14

"He had red hair, and he smiled a lot," Mrs. Wallace said, speaking a little louder than she had spoken to Hoot. "That's about all I remember—that, and he wanted a job."

"And he asked you about the Tolberts," her husband said. "You should've called me as soon as he said that. I was just out back. I'd have heard you."

Mr. Wallace was smaller than his wife. He had a squinty eye and almost no hair at all on top of his head. He'd grown a little deaf over the course of the last few years, which is why his wife hadn't wasted her breath by calling for him.

"He was just looking for a job," Mrs. Wallace said, knowing that now wasn't the time to mention her husband's lack of hearing. "He wasn't like that other fella, the one with the patch over his eye."

Mr. Wallace gave her a disgusted look. "That Ranger fella said to let him know if anybody came by. That means redheaded boys just as much as men with eye patches. The Ranger said it was important."

"You can let the Ranger know, then. It wasn't more than two hours ago that the boy was here."

"I'll let him know, all right," Mr. Wallace said. "If I can find him. I just hope it's not too late."

The Ranger's name was Wilson, and he was in the Salty Dog saloon trying to talk to Kincaid. The place was more crowded than it had been earlier in the day. There was some loud talk and a little laughter now and then. And the piano player had come to work. He was playing "Buffalo Gals" and not missing more than one note out of every five.

Wilson wasn't having much luck with Kincaid, who had been drinking steadily for several hours and had spent just about every penny that he'd gotten from Angel Ware.

"Red hair," Kincaid was saying, or something like that. And then he said something that might have been "big ears."

That would describe Hoot Riley pretty well, Wilson thought, but maybe he could get more from Kincaid if he tried another tactic. So instead of asking questions, he provided a little information.

"The man that was with him," he said. "Did he have long, fair hair? Nearly white?"

"Tha's ri'," Kincaid said. "Looked almos' li' a ang-, ang-, ang-" He couldn't get the word out. Finally he said, "One uh them things with a harp."

"An angel," Wilson said.

"Tha's it. You got it. A sweet li'l ang-, ang-, hell, you know what I'm tryin' to say."

Wilson nodded to show that he knew, but he doubted that Kincaid noticed.

" 'Cept this 'un wasn't so sweet," Kincaid continued. "Tell by 'is eyes. Meaner'n a snake."

That was about as good a description of Angel Ware as Wilson could think of, and there wasn't much doubt in Wilson's mind now that Angel had been the one be-hind the questions asked at the Wallace place. It was a good thing that Mr. Wallace hadn't told Kincaid any-thing useful.

Wilson stood up and flipped a silver dollar onto the table. He watched until Kincaid had managed to corral it by covering it with both hands, then said, "You've been a big help, Mr. Kincaid. But you should be more careful of the company you keep."

Kincaid kept one hand firmly atop the silver dollar, but he moved the other to touch the brow above his good eye, as if to assure himself that the eye was still there.

"Tha's ri'," he said. "Be more careful. Damn sure will. You betcha."

Wilson knew that Kincaid wasn't going to be careful. He was just going to continue to drink for as long as his money lasted. That wasn't Wilson's problem, however. His problem was finding Angel Ware. He pushed his way through the saloon's batwing doors and nearly walked right into Mr. Wallace, who was on his way inside.

Wallace stumbled back, caught himself, and said,

"I'm glad I caught up with you. Somebody else has been by the house asking questions about the Tolberts."

"Who?" Wilson asked.

"Don't know. Some redheaded kid, my wife said. Freckle faced, looked like he was right off the farm. She said he was lookin' for a job and he'd heard the Tolberts needed a hand."

"Who would he have heard that from?" Wilson asked, already knowing the answer. "The Tolberts haven't lived there in a long time."

"That's what the wife told him. But she also told him that the Tolberts had moved down around Blanco."

"Damn," Wilson said, certain that the redhead had been Hoot Riley. "How long ago was that?"

"Two hours or so. I been lookin' for you ever since."

Wilson thanked Wallace and told him that most likely there wouldn't be anyone else coming around to ask questions.

"I'm glad to hear that, then," Wallace said, but Wilson didn't hear him. The Ranger was already half a block away.

By five o'clock that afternoon, Wilson was pretty sure that Angel and Hoot were no longer in town. He'd located the hotel where they'd been staying, not far from the Salty Dog, and the deskman said they'd left a couple of hours earlier.

"Looked like they was in quite a rush," he said. "But I didn't ask 'em why."

Wilson wasn't surprised. He figured that plenty of folks left that particular hotel in a rush.

"I don't guess they mentioned where they were headed," he said.

"Nope," the clerk said. "And I didn't ask 'em. Wasn't any of my business, and besides, they'd paid their bill. All four of 'em."

"Four?"

"That's right. There were the two you asked about and two others."

Wilson asked what the two others had looked like, and the clerk described them. He didn't do a very good job, but Wilson was sure the two were Abilene Jack Sturdivant and Ben Jephson. So they were all still together.

That was all well and good, but it was no longer Wilson's job. He'd been told to check on a bank robbery in Dallas after he'd finished in Fort Worth. There was supposed to be another Ranger already on the way to Blanco. Wilson figured that one Ranger was probably enough against somebody like Angel, but even a Ranger could use a little help now and then. Wilson decided he'd better get off a telegram to what passed for the law in Blanco, let whoever was in charge know what was heading his way.

For a minute or two, Wilson regretted that he wasn't going to Blanco himself. Things were likely to get mighty interesting in those parts before too long.

Chapter 15

Shag Tillman, Blanco's town marshal, didn't like telegrams any better than Brady Tolbert did. His experience had been pretty much like the Ranger's: telegrams brought bad news. You never got one from the governor, telling you what a fine job you were doing. You never got one telling you that some relative you never heard of back East had died and left you a fine home and plenty of money. Instead you usually got one that said some kind of trouble was on the way.

Shag wasn't a man who liked trouble. In fact, he went out of his way to avoid it. He'd never wanted to be the marshal. He'd been perfectly happy to serve as Rawls Dawson's deputy and let Dawson make all the decisions, face any danger that came along, and do most of the work.

But then Dawson had gone and got himself killed, something that Shag didn't plan on having happen to him, not if he could help it. He was going to stay alive just as long as he could, no matter what he had to do, even if that meant passing some of his responsibility along to someone else.

So when he got the telegram, he took it and rode straight out of town to let Ellie Taine know that trouble was on its way and heading in her direction.

Ellie was sitting in the front yard in a swing, enjoying the last of the daylight, when Shag rode up. The sun was reddening the clouds in the west as it dropped down behind them.

"You're just in time for supper," Ellie said, walking out to greet Shag. "Get off your horse and stay awhile."

"No, thank you, ma'am," Shag said. "I won't be stayin' for supper, not that I wouldn't enjoy it, mind you. But I come to bring you some bad news."

He leaned down from his horse and handed her the telegram that he'd received from Fort Worth.

Ellie read it quickly. When she'd finished, she said, "Do you know anything about these men?"

"Nothing but what it says in that telegram," Shag told her. "They're all fresh out of Huntsville prison, and they're likely headed here because your foreman's wife is the sister to one of 'em."

Ellie handed the telegram back to Shag, who reached down and took it.

"We don't know for certain that they're coming here," she said, wishing that she believed it. "They might go anywhere, especially if they know the Texas Rangers are after them."

"Speakin' of the Rangers," Shag said, folding the telegram and sticking it in his shirt pocket, "I ain't seen hide nor hair of the one that it says here is comin' to help us out. He should've been here already, the way it reads."

"Maybe he's here and you just don't know about it."

Shag shook his head sadly. "Now, I know you and some other folks around here don't think I'm much of a lawman, and maybe I'm not. But I keep up with the strangers that come into town. I can name you ever' one that's come in the last two weeks, which ain't many, and not a one of them's a Ranger."

Ellie had to admit to herself that Shag was right about her opinion of his abilities. And of course, she wasn't alone in that opinion. But Shag's shortcomings hadn't mattered much in the past. Blanco wasn't exactly a place where you needed a real gunhand in charge of the peace-keeping. The bank robbery in which her husband had been killed was the only thing like that ever to happen in the area as far as she knew, and she'd lived there all her life.

Because of what Sue Tolbert had told her about Angel Ware, however, Ellie suddenly found herself wishing that Rawls Dawson were still around. Or better even than Rawls, Jonathan Crossland.

But it was no use wishing. They were both dead, and what she had was Shag. And Shag was about as useless as the tits on a boar hog, as her grandfather used to say.

Ellie sighed. "I appreciate you riding all the way out here to let me know about this, Shag."

"Glad to do it," the marshal said. "All a part of the job. But what're we gonna do about it?"

Ellie knew that "we" meant her. Shag had been after

her more than once, asking for her help with some little problem or other that he didn't want to handle on his own. It was all because she'd gone after those rapists and killers who'd robbed the town bank. And because of what had happened when she'd gone after them.

She shook her head. All that was in the past, and it wasn't something she liked to think about. She didn't want to get mixed up in anything like that again.

"These fellas, they wasn't in prison for talkin' back to a sheriff," Shag said. "They're killers. All of 'em. If they come here, they'll cause trouble."

Ellie thought of what Sue had told her about Angel's holding a grudge. Shag could be right about the trouble.

"That Ranger," she said. "The one that's on his way here. Did it say what his name was?"

Shag looked at the telegram. It was getting harder to see as the sunlight faded from the sky.

"Nope. What difference would that make?"

"Lane Tolbert's brother is a Ranger. I thought it might be him."

"Well," Shag said, "I don't care whose brother he is, just as long as he gets here. I don't much like the idea of us havin' to deal with a bunch of killers."

Ellie noted the "us." "They might not come here," she said, knowing that she was wrong.

They'd come, all right. Ellie wasn't one to put much stock in dreams, but it was beginning to look as if Sue's bad dream of a few nights before had been an omen.

"They might, though," Shag said, as if he was reading her mind. "And if they do, you'd better be ready for them."

Ellie pushed her hair back and looked up at him. "We'll be ready," she promised.

But, as it turned out, she was wrong.

PART 2

PART 2

Chapter 16

Sue and Lane were understandably upset when Ellie told them the news about Angel. Or maybe upset was too mild a word. Sue's face twisted as if she might be in pain, and Lane swore.

"He'll come here," Sue said. "I'm sure of it. He'll want to strike back at us. It's the way he is."

"He'd better not," Lane said. "If he does, he'll be sorry. We'll make him sorry."

Ellie felt the same way. She liked the life she had now, and she didn't want anyone upsetting it. More than that, she didn't want anyone she cared about to get hurt.

"He might not come," she said. "He might think it's just not worth the trouble."

"It's worth the trouble to him," Sue said. "You don't know what he's like."

Ellie might not have known, but she was getting the idea. She said, "We'll just have to keep our eyes open. Be on the alert. We can handle him."

Sue shook her head and repeated her earlier statement: "You don't know what he's like."

"You're right," Ellie said, but she was afraid she was going to learn.

They came two nights later, a couple of hours after midnight, when nearly everyone on the ranch was asleep. So much time had passed since the telegram that Ellie had convinced herself they weren't coming at all.

They must have been watching for at least part of the day, because there was a method to their attack. They seemed to know that Ellie was in the big ranch house with Juana, that the Tolberts were in the foreman's house, and that the other hands were in the bunkhouse.

They went straight to the foreman's house and ignored everyone else. They figured to be in and out before anyone really knew what was happening. They almost succeeded, and probably would have, except that Lane Tolbert wasn't really asleep. He was keeping watch, or he had been until he'd dozed off in a chair tipped back against the wall by the bedroom window.

Lane had spent all his life on ranches of one size or another. He wasn't a gunfighter in any sense of the word, but he owned a pistol, as every ranch hand did. You never knew when you'd need to kill a snake, and a man might run across some bad types on the trail, the kind of folks who'd take advantage of an unarmed man but be a little bit shy about bothering a man with a gun.

So that night, as he had for the past couple of nights, Lane had sat up in the chair with his gunbelt hanging within easy reach. If Angel showed up, Lane planned to be ready for him. And he would have been if he hadn't drifted into a light sleep.

But when he heard the noise at the window, it was as if he hadn't been asleep at all.

He sat up straight, bringing all four legs of the chair to the floor, and drew the pistol smoothly from its holster. Then he rolled to his right, out of the chair. He could see a dark figure silhouetted in the window. There was no one on the ranch who had any reason or excuse to be in that place at that time, and with no hesitation at all, Lane pulled the trigger.

The pistol roared. Lane's ears rang, and the muzzle flash blinded him temporarily. He thought he heard Sue screaming, but he wasn't sure. Then something hit him high on the left shoulder. It was as if he'd been kicked by a mule. Two mules.

He fell back against the bed and discovered that he could no longer raise the hand that held the pistol.

And then that he couldn't hold his head up.

And then that he couldn't do anything at all.

As soon as the pistol shot exploded, Sue sat bolt upright in the bed. Something had jolted against the bed, too, and she knew that something was terribly wrong. But she didn't know what. Her first thought was for her daughter.

She jumped out of the bed and stumbled over someone on the floor.

Lane. She knew it was Lane, and that the noise she'd heard had been a gunshot. She wanted to do something for Lane, but she thought of her daughter and ran toward the little room where Laurie slept.

She didn't get there. A man grabbed her. She smelled rotten teeth and sweat, and she clawed at the man's face and screamed.

The man wrapped up her arms and held her close. She twisted and struggled as hard as she could, but he was too strong for her. She knew that she couldn't break his grip, so she bent her head to his shoulder and bit him.

She tasted sweaty cloth, but she hardly noticed. She tried to make her teeth meet through the shirt and the flesh.

The man howled and threw her across the room. She stumbled awkwardly. Her heel caught on something soft, and she fell backward. Her head slammed against the wall, and her teeth clicked together.

That was all she knew.

Laurie, too, was awakened by the gun blast. She sat up straight and called for her mother, but the words had hardly passed her lips before someone clapped a hand over her mouth and said, "Shut up, kid. Your uncle Angel is going to take you for a little ride."

Then she was being lifted and carried away from her bed and outside into the night.

The gunshot roused the men in the bunkhouse, too, but as soon as old Jim Colburn opened the door to see what was happening, he was shot in the leg. There was another shot, but it hit the door frame. Colburn fell back inside the bunkhouse, and no one else tried to go out.

Everyone scrabbled around in the dark and found a weapon, but there wasn't any more shooting. They all figured that as long as they stayed inside and stayed away from the windows, they'd be all right. Since they didn't know for sure what was going on, nobody moved except for Harry Moon, who tried to do something about Colburn's leg. Nobody tried to light a lantern. They had a feeling they'd all be safer in the dark.

Ellie didn't know what was going on, either, but she had a pretty good idea. She found that her mind was perfectly clear, not dulled at all by sleep, and she went straight to the gun cabinet and got out the shotgun that had been Jonathan Crossland's and which now belonged to her. It shot a tight pattern and would be effective even at a little distance.

She would have been just as happy never to pick up a gun again, and in fact she'd tried to avoid it. But there wasn't anything she could do about that now.

She loaded the shotgun with two brass shells and went to the kitchen door. She could hear yelling outside, and there was a second gunshot. Then another one.

Ellie pushed the door open and looked out. The moon was low, and the clouds were thick. All she could make out were some dark forms that looked like men on horseback.

She raised the shotgun and was about to pull a trigger when she heard a girl's muffled scream.

Laurie. Laurie was out there.

Ellie's stomach turned over. She lowered the shotgun. She couldn't take a chance on hitting Laurie.

Someone yelled in an unfamiliar voice, "I'm shot, goddammit! Gimme a hand! I'm shot!"

Ellie walked forward quickly and pointed the shotgun in the direction of the yell. A dark shadow staggered around the corner of the Tolberts' house about ten yards away. In the darkness, Ellie could see that it was a man who seemed to be waving a pistol around feebly.

"I'm shot!" he yelled again.

To make sure he didn't shoot anyone with the pistol, Ellie fired the shotgun.

There was a scream, and Ellie heard the braying of a mule.

"Leave the son of a bitch!" someone yelled, and Ellie heard the churning of hoofbeats.

In only seconds, there was quiet. Ellie counted to thirty. Then she stepped out into the yard.

"Laurie?" she called. "Sue? Lane?"

There was no answer from any of the Tolberts, but Harry Moon yelled to her from the bunkhouse.

"Are they gone, Miss Ellie? We got a wounded man in here."

"They're gone," Ellie said. "Who's hurt?"

Harry came to the bunkhouse door. "Jim Colburn. He's hit in the leg. I don't think he's hurt too bad, though. What happened?"

"I'm not sure. I have to check on the Tolberts."

Ellie's stomach felt as empty and hollow as if she hadn't eaten in weeks. She walked to the foreman's house and saw that the front door was open. The dark shape of a man was lying to one side.

He wasn't moving, and Ellie didn't care whether he was dead or alive. She hardly glanced down at him as she walked by and into the house.

"Laurie? Sue? It's Ellie. Is everything all right?"

There was no answer, and Ellie knew that everything was not all right. She was very afraid that nothing was going to be all right ever again.

Chapter 17

Ellie walked up to the door with the shotgun ready, but there was no need for it, as she saw almost at once. She leaned the gun against the wall and started back to her own house for a light. She'd gone only a couple of steps when Juana came out with a lamp. Ellie waited for Juana to reach her; then they both went into the Tolberts' place.

They found Lane Tolbert lying on the floor of the bedroom. There was blood all over the front of his bare chest. Ellie couldn't tell whether he was breathing or not.

Sue was lying not far away. She was stirring, and her eyes flickered as Ellie bent down to her.

"Go look for Laurie," Ellie told Juana, who stepped into the next room.

"No one is here," Juana called, and Ellie's heart sank, though she'd been expecting it.

"Look under the bed," Ellie said. "Maybe she's hiding."

Ellie helped Sue sit up. Sue's eyes were open, but she wasn't focusing. She opened her mouth to say something, but nothing came out.

"You just sit still," Ellie told her, then turned to Lane.

She put her cheek next to his face and thought that she detected just the faintest exhalation.

"There is no one under the bed," Juana said, coming back into the room. "The little one is gone."

"Go get Mr. Moon," Ellie said, ignoring the hollow feeling in her stomach.

Juana left and Ellie went to Sue, who was now looking around the room. The flickering lamp flame threw jittery shadows on the walls.

"It was Angel, wasn't it," Sue said.

"It must've been," Ellie answered. "I didn't see anyone's face, but I don't know who else it could have been."

Sue's eyes went to Lane's still form. "Is he alive?"

"I don't know. He might be."

"What about Laurie?"

"We can't find her. Do you think she's hiding?"

A tear rolled down Sue's cheek, but her voice was steady. "No. I think he took her."

Harry Moon came into the room with Juana. Moon wasn't a doctor, or anything like it, but he'd proven to have a way with sick animals, and Ellie was hoping his skills might be applied in other situations. He was a short, wiry man with bushy hair and a bristly beard, and he'd put on a pair of denim pants and a wrinkled cotton shirt. Ellie didn't think she'd ever seen him without a hat before.

"Juana tells me somebody's been shot," he said.

"It's Mr. Tolbert," Ellie said. "Will you see if there's anything you can do for him?"

Moon went and knelt down beside Lane. "I've seen a bullet wound or two in my time. Lemme see what we got here." He put his fingers on Lane's neck. "Well, he's still alive, but just barely. I guess I'll have to see just how bad this is, but you and Juana'll have to give me a hand."

Ellie looked at Sue, who said, "I'll be all right. Don't worry about me."

"Just stay here, then," Ellie said, and went to help Moon.

With Ellie and Juana's assistance, Moon raised Lane off the floor and got a look at his back.

"Bullet hit him way up on the shoulder and went straight on through. Made a damn big hole when it came out, though, didn't it. Pardon my language, ladies."

Ellie didn't mind the language. "Is there anything we can do for him?"

"Well, we can put him in the bed, get the bleedin' stopped, and bandage him up, if that's what you mean. After that, we'll just have to trust to luck and the Lord. He's already been mighty lucky. A little bit lower and that bullet might've gone right through his heart."

"So you think he'll live?"

"Hard to say. Probably will if the wound don't get infected. Might be a good idea to pour a little whiskey in there. It'll sting, but he won't feel it."

Ellie sent Juana to the house for some whiskey. Jonathan Crossland had kept a small supply, and Ellie had drunk none of it since his death.

"A little drink might not hurt me, either," Moon said.

"I don't do a whole lot of doctorin'. Might steady my hand."

"Take whatever you want," Ellie said. She turned to Sue. "Lane's going to be fine. Don't you worry about it."

Sue smiled weakly. "I won't."

"That's good, then," Moon said. "Now help me get him on the bed."

An hour later, Sue and Ellie were drinking coffee in Ellie's kitchen. Lane was still in his bed, unconscious, but Moon had assured them that was for the best.

"When he wakes up," Moon said, "he's gonna hurt like hell. Best to let him sleep for as long as he can. I'll sit with him. And leave that whiskey bottle here. It ain't for me. I've had all I need, but I figger he's gonna need a swig when he wakes up."

The man outside, the one both Ellie and Lane had shot, wasn't going to wake up at all. Ellie didn't know who he was, and she didn't really care. He wasn't Angel, and that was all that mattered.

She wasn't sorry she'd killed him, and she wasn't going to waste any grief on him. There'd been a time, not long before, when she might have done so, but she'd changed since then.

She told the men not to bury him. "There's supposed to be a Texas Ranger coming. He'll want to see the body."

"We can't just leave it lyin' here," one of the men

said. His name was Fred Willis, a short, bandy-legged man who could always see the worst side of any situation. "It'll mortify on us. Liable to poison us all."

"If the Ranger's not here by tomorrow at noon, you can bury it. Now, who wants to ride into town and let Marshall Tillman know what's happened?"

"I'll go," said Willis. "He won't like me gettin' him out of bed, though."

Ellie didn't care what Shag liked. "Just tell him to come. It's his job."

Fred had nothing to say to that. He went to saddle his horse, and Ellie went to get Sue.

"Are you sure Lane will be all right?" Sue asked. "Harry Moon's a good man, but he's no doctor."

"He's the closest thing to a doctor we have, though," Ellie said, sipping the steaming coffee. "We don't have a real doctor in Blanco anymore. We'll just have to pray that Lane comes through this. It's Laurie I'm worried about."

Sue's steady gaze faltered. "So am I. I should have known that something like this would happen. Angel always has to get revenge, and of course he'd want to do the thing that would hurt me most. He wouldn't kill me. That wouldn't give him any satisfaction. He'd take away what I loved most and leave me alive to suffer."

"He didn't take Lane."

"That's right, but it wasn't for lack of trying. He wanted to kill him. He just missed."

Ellie's stomach turned over at the word "kill." "You don't think he'll kill Laurie."

"No. He wouldn't do that. Not for a while. He'll keep her alive as long as he thinks I'm grieving. Or until he gets tired of her."

"How long will that take?" Ellie asked.

Sue shook her head. "It won't take long. He gets tired of things pretty quickly."

"Those men with him wouldn't let him kill a little girl."

Sue took a deep breath and let it out slowly. She tried to take a sip of coffee, but her hand was shaking too hard. She set the mug back down.

"Those men are probably no better than Angel," she said. "They might even be worse."

Ellie knew she was right.

"What are we going to do, Ellie?" Sue asked. There was a sob in her voice. "We can't let Angel kill my baby."

"There's a Texas Ranger coming," Ellie said.

"When? You told me he was coming two days ago, and he's not here yet. What if he doesn't come at all? And what will he do when he gets here? Angel will be long gone by then. He may even have killed Laurie."

"No, he won't. He won't kill anyone."

"Who's going to stop him?"

"We are," Ellie said.

Chapter 18

❖⊱⊰❖

It was just after daylight when Fred Willis and Shag Tillman got to the ranch, which Shag still thought of as "the Crossland place." It didn't seem right to him that a woman owned it now, even though she was a hell of a woman, no doubt about that. He wondered what Fred thought about working for a woman, but he didn't ask. He thought he knew the answer anyhow, since the woman was Ellie Taine.

"Where's that dead man you were tellin' me about?" he asked instead.

"Right out by the Tolberts' house," Fred answered. "Got a bullet hole in him. Took on a load of buckshot, too."

"Who shot him?"

"I didn't ask, but the pistol shot, I reckon that was Mr. Tolbert. The shotgun, now, that must've been Miss Ellie. Wasn't anybody else could've done it."

Shag wasn't surprised. Anybody who messed with Ellie Taine was making a big mistake. You could ask those fellas who robbed the bank about that, except that you'd have to dig them up to ask, and that wouldn't work because they were just too damn dead to answer.

Thinking about Ellie sometimes shamed the marshal, because he knew that she had something he lacked. Call it what you wanted to, nerve or gumption or grit, Shag had just never had a whole lot of it. He liked for everyone to behave, not cause any trouble, keep everything nice and calm and peaceful. When things went wrong, he was generally at a loss, and those times always made him wonder how he'd ever gotten talked into pinning on a badge in the first place.

But Ellie Taine, well, she was different, which is why Shag figured Fred would have said he didn't mind working for her at all. She wasn't what you'd call a handsome woman, but she had plenty of backbone. Truth to tell, Shag knew deep down that even if she was a woman, she was a better man than he was, not that he'd ever say that to anybody.

Fred showed Shag the body, still lying right where it had fallen.

After receiving the telegram from Fort Worth, Shag had looked through the most recent batch of wanted posters for the four men the Ranger had mentioned. The one on the ground matched the description of Abilene Jack Sturdivant.

Shag told Fred the dead man's name. "Killed three men in a saloon fight down around Galveston. Shot one of 'em in the back, killed two of 'em with his bare hands. It all started with an argument over some woman. He was a mean one."

Shag stared down at the body. The blood had congealed around the bullet hole in the stomach and the buckshot wound that had taken out a chunk of Sturdivant's chest. The flies had found it. They were buzzing around, and there was a rank smell that made Shag turn his head.

Fred said, "Wasn't as rough as he thought he was, looks like. Not as rough as Miss Ellie, anyhow. And he's mortifyin' already. We need to plant him quick."

"No need to take him into town," Shag said. "Just put him under somewhere out here if you can spare the space."

Fred gave a short laugh. "That's one thing we got plenty of. I don't reckon Miss Ellie would mind, not as long as we don't bury him too near to Mr. Crossland."

"We can ask her. Where is she?"

"In the house, most likely. Harry's supposed to be sittin' with Mr. Tolbert."

Shag dismounted.

I'll see to your horse," Fred said.

Shag thanked him and went into the house. There was no one in the kitchen but Juana, who was washing dishes in a big pan. Shag could smell bacon and coffee. He couldn't decide which smelled better.

"Where's Miss Ellie?" Shag asked, taking off his hat and holding it in front of him.

Juana wiped her hands on her spotless white apron. "She is gone."

Shag didn't like that answer. He was almost afraid to ask his next question, but he knew he had to do it.

"Gone where?"

"She went after the men who came here. The men took Señora Tolbert's little girl with them, and Señora Taine is going to get her back."

Oh, Lord, thought Shag.

"Señora Taine said to tell you that you were not to worry about her. She said that she and Señora Tolbert will be just fine."

Shag didn't say anything, but he started to sweat. He could feel it trickling down his side.

"She also said to tell you that if the Texas Ranger comes, he should go and look for them. But you do not need to send a posse."

Sure, Shag thought. *But if I don't, and if I'm not the one leading it, what'll that make me look like to everybody in town?* He wiped sweat off his upper lip.

"She said that I should offer you breakfast," Juana went on. "Fresh eggs and bacon. Good strong coffee."

Shag's stomach was churning. A moment before, he'd been quite hungry, but he couldn't possibly eat now, not the way he was feeling. His appetite had completely disappeared.

On the other hand, he wasn't in any hurry to go back to town. Maybe if he took his time, the Ranger would be there when he got back. Shag had told his deputy where he was going, and maybe the deputy would send the Ranger on to the Crossland place, and then he'd take charge.

If things worked out like that, Shag wouldn't have to worry about the posse or anything else. He wouldn't be responsible any longer. Thinking about it that way, he began to feel a whole lot better. He even felt a little hungry again. And he always liked a cup of hot coffee in the morning. He hadn't had time for one when Fred Willis had come to get him.

"How would those eggs be fixed?" he asked.

"How would you like them?"

"Scrambled."

"Then they would be scrambled."

"With a little cheese and onion in 'em?"

"Sí. I can do that if you wish."

"Well, I guess I could spare the time to eat, seein' as how that's the way Miss Ellie wants it. I'll just go out and see how the boys are doin' with that body in the yard."

He needed to tell them to go ahead and bury Sturdivant. There was no use in letting the body lie around, and he didn't think Ellie would be back anytime soon.

"The food will be ready quickly," Juana said.

"What I have to do won't take long," Shag said. "It won't take long at all."

Chapter 19

Laurie was riding behind her uncle Angel with both arms around his waist. She didn't like the way Uncle Angel smelled, and she didn't like the way he laughed. It was a mean kind of laugh, and it didn't sound as if he really thought anything was funny.

She didn't like the red-haired man named Hoot, either. He was singing "Buffalo Gals" as loud as he could, but he didn't have a nice voice, and now and then he would look at her in a way that made her feel uncomfortable, though she couldn't have explained exactly why.

The other man, Ben, was different. He rode along a little behind the others, and he hadn't said more than two or three words all morning. Laurie wondered if maybe he was sick.

"I want to go back home," she said.

Angel laughed his laugh that wasn't really a laugh. Then he said, "I've already told you all about that, honey. You haven't seen your uncle Angel in a long time, and we're going to have us a picnic to celebrate. It'll be fun."

"I'm not having fun," Laurie said. "I want my clothes."

She was uncomfortable, being outside in her nightgown. It wasn't made for riding, and it was hiked up too high. She didn't like being barefoot, either. She needed some riding britches, some boots, and a hat.

Hoot stopped singing. "You won't need any clothes, little lady. Trust your uncle Hoot."

"You're not my uncle," Laurie told him.

He gave her one of those looks she didn't like. "I'm sure not, honey. I'm sure not."

She didn't like the way he said "honey." It made her skin feel bumpy.

"Where are we going to have a picnic?" she asked Angel.

"It's not far now. It's a nice place."

"Why didn't my mother come? And what about my father?"

"Now, you don't need to worry about them. They know you'll be safe with me."

He laughed again, and this time it did sound as if he thought something was funny. Laurie couldn't figure out what it could be.

"Why did you wrap me up in that blanket?" she asked.

"It was just part of the fun. I thought you'd enjoy it."

Laurie hadn't enjoyed it. The blanket had smelled horsey and it had made her sneeze. There hadn't been anything fun about it.

There hadn't been anything fun about the noises she'd heard, either. She was sure they'd been gunshots, but she was afraid to ask Angel about them. She was afraid of what he might say, because she knew that something was very wrong.

She had always liked her uncle when he visited in the past, but she could tell that her mother and father were uncomfortable when he was around. They never said so, but Laurie sensed that they were. Now she was beginning to think that she knew why, and what she thought was scaring her a little bit.

She wasn't going to tell Angel what she thought, however. She didn't want him to know she was afraid.

Besides, she told herself, she *wasn't* afraid, not really afraid. Her father wouldn't want her to be afraid, and neither would her mother and Miss Ellie.

"Are we going back home after the picnic?" she asked.

"Not right after," Angel said. "We're going to camp out for a while. You'll like it. We'll have us a real campfire and sleep out under the stars."

"I don't like sleeping out under the stars," Laurie said, though she really had no idea what it would be like. She'd never slept outside before. Riding behind her uncle through the darkness hadn't been fun, however, and she didn't think anything would be fun with him around.

There had been a time when she liked him. He'd tried to please her and made her laugh. But he seemed different now, different in a way that Laurie couldn't explain but that she didn't like at all.

"I don't much care whether you like it or not," Angel said, and there was something hard and cold in his voice that Laurie had never heard there before. "You're going to do what I tell you, and that's all you need to worry about."

"Don't worry, little honey," Hoot said. "I won't let him hurt you."

"You can keep your mouth shut," Angel told him.

Laurie looked at Hoot, who seemed to want to say something, but who laughed instead and rode on ahead of them. He started singing again.

Laurie closed her eyes and promised herself that whatever happened, she wasn't going to cry.

Nothing about what had happened made sense to Jephson. He'd tried to let Abilene Jack convince him that Angel was after money, though he'd never really believed it. Now Abilene Jack was dead, and it didn't make a damn bit of difference what either of them believed.

Nevertheless, Jephson wished that Jack were there to talk to. He'd like to ask him what he thought was going on. Jephson had tried and tried to figure it out, but no matter how he put the parts together, nothing fit right.

They'd left Fort Worth and ridden down to Blanco, where Angel's sister lived. Angel kept telling them that he wanted to visit his family, but when they'd arrived at the ranch where she was living, Angel changed his story. Now he said that he was going to steal his sister's daughter.

When Jephson had asked why, Angel had said, "Because I want to, and because she'll know it was me that took the kid, that's why."

It wasn't any kind of an answer as far as Jephson was concerned.

"I think you ought to tell us more than that," he said.

"Remember Hob Bowman?" Angel said. "And how I told you that one day I'd get back at him?"

Jephson said that he remembered. He wasn't likely to forget Hob Bowman.

"Well," Angel told him, "it took me a while, but I did what I said. And now I'm gonna do it to my sister. Nobody can treat me the way she did and get away scot-free."

Jephson could understand that Angel wanted revenge, but he didn't like the idea of being dragged in on it. It was bad enough that they'd killed Bowman and the others. This looked to be even worse. But he didn't see what he could do about it. He'd gotten in too deep to back out now.

Angel had watched the place where his sister lived for a few hours, and when he'd worked out a plan, he told them what he wanted them to do. Jephson hadn't understood that, either.

"I don't care whether you understand it or not," Angel told him. "You just do what I tell you, and we'll get along fine. If you don't want to do it, light a shuck on out of here. I sure as hell don't need you."

At that point Jephson had shut his mouth. He'd still thought he needed Angel, whether Angel needed him or not. Now he wasn't so sure.

And now there was something else he didn't like: Leaving Jack back there hadn't been right. Maybe Jack was dead, but maybe he wasn't. They didn't know that for sure. They should at least have tried to see if there was anything to be done for him, but Angel wouldn't hear of it.

Jephson was a little ashamed that he'd let Angel bully him like that. He could have ignored him, but he was afraid to, so Jack was still back there, dead or alive, and Jephson didn't have him to talk to anymore.

And later he'd overheard Hoot asking Angel about what happened in the house. There'd been a shot fired, but Angel wouldn't talk about it. Jephson wondered if someone had been killed. What if it was the girl's mother or father? That was the kind of thing Angel would like, all right. It would fit right in with his idea of getting back at somebody.

There were a couple of other things bothering Jephson as well. He didn't like it that they'd taken the girl, and didn't like lying to her about some picnic.

It wasn't as if the girl meant anything to him, Jephson told himself. But the way Hoot kept looking at her scared him. He'd seen a starving coyote look at a dead rabbit that way once.

And Jephson didn't like the tone of Angel's voice when he talked to the girl. It didn't sound like the way an uncle talked to his close kin. It sounded more like an executioner talking to a condemned prisoner.

Jephson looked around him. He'd never been in this

part of the state before, and it was mighty pretty country, especially early in the morning with the sun reddening the sky in the east. It would have been even prettier if he'd been in a mood to enjoy it, which he wasn't.

It didn't look like farming country. It was just too rocky, but there were trees all around, pecan, elm, hackberry, and even some walnut. He'd seen a few deer back in the trees at just about dawn, and there were rabbits and armadillos all around. But there wasn't any sign of a town. They'd skirted Blanco and left it behind them hours earlier. Jephson wondered just where in the hell they were going and what Angel was planning to do.

He rode up beside Angel, leading the mule that Abilene Jack had been riding, and said, "Where are we headed for this picnic of yours?"

"Where are we headed?" Angel said. "You probably won't believe me when I tell you."

"Try me."

"Church," Angel said. "We're goin' to church."

Chapter 20

The Ranger arrived just as Shag Tillman was finishing his breakfast. He was a big man with black hair and even blacker eyes. His skin was brown as saddle leather.

Shag stood and greeted him.

"Glad to meet you, Marshal," the Ranger said. "My name's Brady Tolbert."

It was a wonder how a good meal could change a man's outlook on things. Shag was feeling mighty good now, not worried at all about what was going to happen.

He felt even better as he shook hands with the Ranger. There was something about a big man with a badge that he'd carved himself out of a silver ten-peso piece that made you feel like everything was going to turn out just fine.

Shag's good feeling didn't last long, however. That changed when he explained the situation and the Ranger said that he wanted to see his brother.

"Your brother?" Shag said.

"Like I said, my name's Brady Tolbert. When I met your deputy in town, he said that a man named Lane Tolbert had been shot out here. Lane's my brother."

"Damn. I'm sorry about that. I didn't know. I should've guessed from your name."

"No reason to feel bad about it. Just tell me where he is, and how he's doing."

"I'll just take you to him," Shag said.

Lane was still sleeping. Harry Moon was sitting in a chair by the bed. He had the chair tilted on its back legs, with his feet up on the window frame. He was chewing tobacco and looking out the window.

Shag told Harry the Ranger's name and said, "That's his brother."

Harry thumped the chair down on all four legs, stood up, and shook hands with Brady. Then he worked his chew around so that he could talk.

"Your brother's doin' pretty good. Might have a little fever, but not as much as you'd think. He's a strong man. He'll get through this just fine."

"What about a doctor?"

"Don't have one in Blanco," Shag said. "We used to, still do, I guess you could say, but only in a manner of speakin'. He got to likin' his own medicine so much that he's not much use to anybody. Just lies around in a daze most of the time."

"A doctor couldn't do anything more for your brother than I've done," Moon said. "Miss Ellie and I took good care of him."

Brady looked at the neat bandage and hoped that Moon was right. Well, he couldn't do anything about it right now, other than hope for the best. As Moon had said, Lane was a strong man, and he was on his own for the time being. Brady had other problems to deal with.

From what the marshal had told him, Angel Ware and two of his men were on the loose with Brady's niece, and Sue and the woman who owned the ranch had gone after her. Now he was going have to go after all of them. He told Tillman that they'd need a posse.

"You can go back to town and get it together while I talk to the folks here a little bit more," Brady told him. "I'll meet you in town, and then we can ride out."

"I thought all you Texas Rangers liked to work alone," Shag said.

"Sometimes we do, but not when we're going up against three known killers with a hostage. And not when two women are out there on the trail looking for the killers. God knows what might happen to them if they actually catch up to Angel Ware."

Shag started to say that he didn't think anything was going to happen to them because Ellie Taine could take care of herself just as well as any man. He also thought about saying that if anybody was in trouble, it was Angel Ware, but he didn't. The Ranger might think he was joking.

"I might better stay in town," he said. "Those old boys might circle around and come back here."

"You can leave your deputy in charge," Brady said. "I don't think you have to worry about Angel coming back."

Shag could see that it wasn't likely he was going to be able to get out of doing his job, but he gave it one more try.

"I'm not sure how many men I can round up for a posse. There's not a lot of folks living in Blanco. They all got jobs to do."

"We don't need many men. Maybe some of the ranch hands would ride with us."

"How many men you need?" Harry asked.

"Two or three's plenty. I don't like riding with too many men. Too many things can go wrong."

"Well, then," Harry said. "There ain't no need for Shag to go back into town. We got that many men right here. I'll go, and I'll bet Fred'll want to go along soon as the boys get back from buryin' that fella Miss Ellie killed. We all think a whole lot of Mr. Tolbert, and we'd like to set things right for him if we can."

"Who's going to stay with my brother?" Brady asked.

"Juana can sit with him. She keeps house and cooks for Miss Ellie, and she can take care of your brother as good as I could. Maybe better."

Shag knew he was whipped. There was no way he was going to get out of going after those killers, so he might as well make the best of things.

"That's settled, then," he said to Brady. "You can ask your questions, and as soon as Fred gets back we can get on the trail. I'll see if Juana can spare us some supplies."

"See if she'll fix us some of those hot tamales of hers," Moon said. "I dearly love those hot tamales with beans."

"I'm not askin' her for any special favors," Shag told him. "If you want hot tamales, you'll have to ask for 'em yourself."

"I'll just do that," Harry said. "And I'll send her on out here when she's done."

"Fine," Brady said. "Let me have a few minutes with my brother, and then I'll be ready. Since you and this Fred fella are going along, I won't have to question anyone here. I can find out what I need to know as we ride."

"Sounds good to me," Moon said.

He went outside, and Shag followed him.

"What do you think of that Ranger?" Shag asked when they were nearing the house.

"Looks like he can take care of hisself to me. I'll be proud to ride with him."

"I guess I will, too," Shag said.

He didn't really mean it, though. The only place he wanted to ride was straight back to Blanco. He was pretty sure that if he went after the men who'd shot Lane Tolbert and stolen his daughter, he might never ride back to Blanco again.

He wiped sweat off his upper lip and said, "Those fellas never thought twice about shootin' Mr. Tolbert, did they."

"Hell, no," Moon said. "I doubt they thought about it once. Folks like that don't think. They just *do*."

That's my trouble, Shag thought. *I spend too much time thinkin' about what's goin' to happen to me. Maybe if I could think less, I could do more.*

"You reckon you're gonna be able to talk Juana out of any of those hot tamales?" he asked.

"You never can tell," Moon said.

Brady looked down at his sleeping and feverish brother.

"I'll see what I can do about gettin' your wife and daughter back, Lane," he said aloud.

He'd heard somewhere that sometimes sick people who seemed to be asleep could hear what was being said to them and even understand it. He didn't know whether that was so or not, but he wanted to give Lane whatever comfort he could.

"This time, we'll put Angel so far back in that prison, he'll never see the light of day again, I promise you that. You'll never have to worry about him coming around you and yours again."

He thought he saw Lane's eyelids flutter as if in agreement, but that could have been just his imagination.

Chapter 21

＊━━✦━━＊

Ellie Taine had been doing a lot of riding since inheriting the ranch, so she was in much better shape than the last time she'd headed out to look for men who'd done her wrong.

She remembered how it had been that time, how her blood had been boiling for revenge. The thing that bothered her about it was that revenge wasn't all it had been cracked up to be.

This time it was different. Ellie wasn't after revenge. She was going after someone who'd taken someone who mattered to her.

Maybe it wasn't that way for Sue. Maybe Sue wanted to get back at her brother for what he'd done to her, to her husband, to their daughter. If that was the way she felt, Ellie was sure she'd change her mind before long. Sue was a smart woman, and she learned quickly. She wasn't like her brother, who still seemed to believe that revenge was something worth waiting for, worth killing for. He'd never learned the lesson that Ellie had.

Well, he was about to, if Ellie had anything to say about it.

"How do you know they're headed this way?" Sue asked as they passed along a stand of hackberry and pecan trees with bright green leaves.

Sue already looked tired to Ellie. She wasn't as used to riding as Ellie was, and Ellie knew that the day was going to be hard on her. It was already hot, and the sun hadn't been up much more than a couple of hours.

"I know a little about tracking," Ellie said. "I learned a few things from Mr. Crossland a while before he died."

Ellie had learned more than a little, but it wasn't something she liked to talk about. She hadn't told Sue much of the story, and Sue had been too polite to ask. But Ellie was sure Sue had heard most of it. People around Blanco were no different from people anywhere else. They all liked to talk.

In fact, if Ellie knew anything about human nature, Sue had probably heard a mighty exaggerated version of what had happened, which might explain why Sue had been so ready to go with her when she proposed that they get Laurie back themselves. Sue might've gotten the impression that Ellie was some kind of one-woman gang.

"Where could they be going?" Sue asked. "What's out here?"

"Nothing that I can think of except the river," Ellie said. "They might be going down to San Antonio. They might even be headed for the border."

She was sorry the second she said it, but it was too late to take it back.

"The border? You mean they might take Laurie into Mexico? We'd never find them there! We can't let that happen."

"We won't. We'll catch up to them a long time before they get there."

"And what will we do when we catch up to them?" Sue asked, her eyes wild. "I don't know why we did this, Ellie. We must have been crazy."

"We did it because we both love Laurie, and we didn't have anybody else to do it, that's why. We aren't crazy."

"We should have sent for the marshal. He would have know what to do."

"Shag Tillman?" Ellie asked. "He barely knows how to saddle a horse."

She realized that she wasn't being fair. Shag was a good man, and he wanted to do the right thing. It was just that he didn't want to risk getting hurt while he was doing it, and that was an attitude that Ellie didn't understand.

If you got hurt, what did it matter, as long as you were doing the right thing? And she knew they were doing the right thing.

"I should have made you wait for the Ranger," Sue said, apparently forgetting that she was the one who'd questioned whether the Ranger would ever arrive. "We're just two women. What can we do?"

"You might be surprised."

"I've heard the stories about you," Sue said, confirming Ellie's suspicion. "But I'm not like you. I can't do the kind of things you did."

"Most of what you heard probably wasn't true, and the rest was likely overstated a little bit. Maybe more than a little bit. But I can tell you from experience that you might be surprised at what you can do when you have to."

"I don't think so. I'm too worried about Lane. And about Laurie. About what Angel might do to her."

"He's not going to do a thing to her," Ellie said, surprised by the savage tone of her voice. "We're not going to let him."

Sue gave her a startled look.

"I love that little girl," Ellie said. "And nobody's going to hurt her."

"I believe you," Sue said, and smiled for the first time that day.

It wasn't much of a smile, but it encouraged Ellie.

"I'm glad you believe me. Now, I think we'd better stop and rest for a while. I don't know about you, but I can't sit in this saddle much longer."

"You're just saying that because you know how I feel."
And how's that?"

"Like someone was trying to break me in two like a wishbone. It's been too long since I spent any time on a horse."

"I feel the same way. That's why we need to stop."

"I won't argue. It's just that I hate to think of Angel getting farther and farther away from us."

"You don't have to worry about that. He's going to have to stop to rest, too, even if he is riding a mule."

"A mule?"

"I heard one bray when he was making his getaway. So

someone's riding one. Maybe him. Maybe all of them. Mules are good animals, but we can keep up with them. And there's another thing. He won't be expecting us, so he won't be ready when we do catch up with him. So you just put your mind at rest."

"I don't think I can do that."

"Well, you can try. Now, let's get off these horses for a while."

The sun was already getting bright, so they rode into the shade of the trees. A squirrel skittered across some dry leaves and ran up a tree trunk.

Ellie drank from her canteen, put the top back on, then stared up into the treetops. She looked back down and said, "You really don't think your brother would do anything to Laurie, do you? She's his blood kin."

"Her being kin wouldn't matter to Angel," Sue said. "I don't think he cares about anyone except maybe himself, and sometimes I'm not even sure of that."

"I can't understand a man like that."

"I don't think anybody can." Sue paused. "You really care about Laurie, don't you."

"As much as if she were my own."

"I thought so. If anything should happen to me —"

"Nothing's going to happen to you," Ellie said. "Or to me, either. Let's get back on the trail."

They mounted up and rode out of the trees, heading in the direction of the river.

Chapter 22

There wasn't much left of the old church. The boards were weathered to a light gray, and a lot of the roof was gone. There were bird nests way up in the rafters, and the windows were just empty holes. The church was surrounded and shaded by tall sycamore trees, their leaves hanging motionless in the stillness of the day. The whole building sagged a little to one side, as if it had begun settling into a hole, though there was no hole there.

On the north side there was a little cemetery, overgrown with grass and weeds. Once there had been a fence around it, but the fence was long gone. There were a few weathered headstones sticking up here and there, but the others had tumbled over and were half buried in the soil.

The only good thing about the place, as far as Jephson could see, was the fact that it wasn't far from the banks of the river. He couldn't see the river from where they were because of all the trees, but he knew it was there. He could hear it running over the limestone rocks.

"Goddamn," Hoot said, giving the old building the once-over. "That sure ain't much of a church."

Angel looked at him with eyes as flat as glass. "I don't want you talkin' that way in front of my niece."

"Talkin' what way?"

"You know what I mean," Angel said.

"Oh, hell. I didn't say nothin' she hadn't heard before. Did I, little lady?"

Angel rode his mule over beside Hoot. One second Angel's knife was in his boot, the next it was in his hand, its point touching the soft flesh under Hoot's chin.

"This is my niece here with me on this mule," Angel said. "And that over there is a church. I don't want to have to tell you again about usin' the wrong kind of language."

Hoot laughed shakily. "Sure Angel. It's just that I've been in pri—"

Before he could get the word out, Angel jerked his hand upward, forcing the point of the knife through a layer or two of Hoot's skin. Laurie saw the bright blood pop out, and she said, "Stop, Uncle Angel, stop!"

Angel relaxed slightly and moved the knife slightly downward.

"Sorry to scare you, honey. I was just tryin' to teach Mr. Hoot some manners."

To Hoot he said, "It's not always smart to talk about where you've been spendin' your time."

The point of the knife was still less than an inch from Hoot's chin. A trickle of blood ran down his neck and into his shirt.

He said, "I see what you mean, Angel. I surely do. I'll watch myself from now on."

"You do that," Angel said, and the knife disappeared into his boot. It was there one instant, gone the next.

Jephson watched the whole thing, not saying a word but feeling more and more as if he'd made a mistake that was far too late to undo. He even wished, briefly, that he'd done things differently, that he'd done something, anything, to help Hob Bowman. But there was nothing he could have done. He'd been chained to Angel then, and he was chained to him now. The chains were different, and you couldn't even see them, but they were there just the same.

"What kind of a place is this?" he asked Angel.

"Like I said, it's a church. There used to be a little settlement not far from here, and the folks there built them a church here in this grove of trees. Then there was a fire that took the whole settlement, burned ever' house in it, and people were so discouraged they didn't try to build it back. The church house, bein' out of the way like it was, didn't get burned. So they just left it."

"The settlement lasted long enough for a few folks to die," Hoot said, looking at the tumbled gravestones.

"Some of 'em died in the fire," Angel said. "There was nowhere else to take 'em to be buried."

Jephson looked over his shoulder. The sky in the west was turning dark blue, almost purple.

"Rain comin'," he said. "Looks like a bad one."

As far as he was concerned, the rain was welcome. He

knew there were people on their trail by now, and a good hard rain would wash out any tracks the mules had left.

On the other hand, something about the decaying church spooked him, and he didn't much like the idea of being around it for too long. He knew he was just being superstitious, but that didn't change the way he felt.

"We'll just ride around back," Angel said. "We can leave the mules there while we have us a little picnic inside."

"You right sure we oughta stop here?" Hoot asked. "There's bound to be a po—"

He clapped his mouth shut before he got the word out. Angel was already riding toward him, knife in hand.

"I talk too much," Hoot said hastily. "I don't mean nothin' by it."

It was becoming clear to Jephson that Angel didn't want his niece to know anything about her uncle's prison time or the fact that there was undoubtedly a posse after them. But that didn't change the fact that Hoot was right. Their best bet was to keep on the move. If they stopped now, they'd be giving the posse a good chance to catch up with them. The more miles they traveled with the rain washing out their tracks, the better, or so it seemed to Jephson.

He started to say something along those lines to Angel, but Angel got in the first word.

"We're gonna stop here and have a little picnic. I don't want Laurie gettin' wet if she doesn't have to. Her mama and daddy'd never forgive me if she got wet and caught a cold."

Jephson didn't think Angel gave a cuss one way or the other whether Laurie caught a cold, and he knew damn well that Angel didn't care what Laurie's parents thought. But he didn't want Angel pulling that knife on him, so he kept his thoughts to himself.

Angel rode his mule around the graveyard, and Hoot followed him. Jephson rode along behind, leading the spare mule. It was cool under the trees, and a little breeze sprang up, riffling the leaves.

"Looks like that rain'll be here before you know it," Angel said. "We'd better get inside."

The inside of the church didn't look to Jephson as if it promised much protection from the rain. There were holes in the roof big enough to throw a saddle through, and the floor was covered with dead leaves from the trees outside.

The pews and the altar were gone, and there was no sign of a piano. There was trash scattered around, some cans and paper that made it obvious to Jephson that the church had been used as a camping place more than once by people who happened on it while on the trail.

Hoot threw his saddle on the floor, looked around, and started singing "Jesus Loves Me."

"I know that song," Laurie said, and she sang along with Hoot on the chorus.

When they had finished, she said to Hoot, "Do you know about Jesus?"

Hoot laughed. "Honey," he said, "Jesus wouldn't have a thing to do with a fella like me. The closest to Him I'll ever come is bein' around an Angel." He laughed at his joke, then sat down with his back to the wall and leaned against it. "Why don't you come over here and sit by me for a little while, honey. We could sing some more songs."

"I don't want to sit by you. You smell like a pig."

Angel laughed, and Hoot's face turned so red that Jephson couldn't see his freckles.

"She's right, Hoot," Angel said. "You might oughta clean yourself up now and then."

Hoot didn't say a thing, but he gave Laurie a look from under his hat brim that frightened Jephson. It had both hate and desire mixed in it, and Jephson thought of that coyote again.

"Now, then," Angel said. "Let's see what we have for that picnic."

He set a pair of saddlebags on the floor and began to empty them as if he didn't have a thing in the world to worry about. Maybe he had some secret that the others didn't know, Jephson thought. He wished to hell he could figure out what it was.

But he forgot about it when the wind started to blow. It came whistling through the cracks in the walls and rushing in through the window openings. Leaves scratched and scattered all over the floor.

Angel looked around and said, "We can stay out

of the wind in the corner over there, and I think the roof's solid up above it. Might as well make ourselves comfortable."

Jephson moved toward the corner, pretty sure that he was never going to be comfortable again.

Chapter 23

❊❊❊

Brady Tolbert was thinking about his brother and how
their lives had been completely different. Lane was two
years older, and he'd always been the more serious of the
two. He was quiet and studious, liked to read, and even
liked to do arithmetic problems. He'd gotten married and
settled down almost as soon as he was able, while Brady
had banged around and tried a couple of different jobs before deciding that he wanted to ride with the Texas
Rangers.

Their parents had always worried that Brady would
come to a bad end, and they'd been very happy when he'd
become a Ranger. That was a job they could respect and
understand, even if there was a certain amount of danger
in it.

They hadn't worried about Lane, but then they hadn't
known about Angel Ware.

Brady thought it was funny, though not the laughing
kind of funny, that Lane was the one whose life was in
jeopardy, through no real fault of his own. If he and Sue

hadn't turned Angel in, they wouldn't have had any trouble with him when he escaped from prison. But they'd done the right thing, and now they were paying for it.

It was also funny that while Lane had been the one to take care of Brady for most of their growing up, he was the one who needed taking care of now. It sure hadn't been that way when they were kids. Whenever anyone had picked on his little brother, Lane was right there to take up for him.

Brady recalled the time that Lew Wickliff jumped him because of something that Brady had said. He had taken Brady by surprise and had him facedown on the ground, sitting on his back and rubbing his face in the dirt.

It was Lane who'd pulled Lew off Brady's back and held him until Brady could get to his feet and paw the dirt out of his eyes and nose.

"I'm gonna let you go now," Lane said to Lew. "And then you two can have at it as long as you want to. But this time it's gonna be a fair fight."

Lew hadn't been looking for a fair fight, but he hadn't run away from it. Brady bloodied his nose for him and blacked one of his eyes before he called calf-rope.

That had been more than twenty years before, but Brady remembered it as if it had happened yesterday. Lane hadn't been worried about Brady getting whipped. Whether he did or not didn't matter to Lane. He just wanted it to be a fair fight. That was all he ever asked for.

Now it was Brady's turn to take care of Lane, but Brady hadn't been there to help him when the time came.

There was nothing he could do about it. It was just bad luck. But because Brady had been delayed, Lane had been shot in what Brady was damn sure wasn't a fair fight. Not that there was anything Brady could do about it.

Well, there was one thing. He could make sure that Angel Ware paid the price for what he'd done.

It wasn't going to be all that easy, however. Not only had Angel got clean away, Lane's wife and another woman were out there looking for him. Brady didn't like the idea of having someone in his way when the shooting started. He hoped that he and his posse got to Angel before they did.

He was a little doubtful about his posse. Willis and Moon seemed like good men, but they were cowhands, not gunfighters. If they'd fired their pistols at all, it was probably to shoot at a rabbit, and just to scare it.

Shag Tillman was a lawman, but that didn't mean much. He didn't seem to be exactly champing at the bit to find Angel. In fact, it seemed to Brady that Tillman was reluctant even to get on the trail.

And now that it looked like rain, Tillman was asking if they shouldn't turn back.

"Hard enough to track anybody on this rocky ground even when it's dry," he said. "If it comes up a good hard rain, we won't be able to find a sign of them. The truth of the matter is, we might as well turn back, maybe come out lookin' again tomorrow if it clears off."

There was a thick black cloud out to the west, and it was moving in on them fast. It was going to rain, all right, but Brady wasn't going to let a little rain, or even a lot of it stop him. He was about to say so, but Moon beat him to it.

"You ain't gonna melt if you get wet," he told Shag. "We got a boss man lyin' back there with a bullet wound, and we got a little girl out here somewhere with a pack of killers. What kinda men would we be if we turned back?"

Brady had tried not to think too much about Laurie. There was no telling what Angel had in mind for her. It didn't bear much thinking about.

Tillman shrugged. "I was just sayin' that it ain't gonna be easy to find a trail. We could ride around out here for a week and not see a sign of anybody."

"We'll find 'em," Willis said. "I don't figure there could be too many places out here for them to hide."

"What about Miss Ellie and Miz Tolbert?" Shag said. "What're we gonna do about them?"

Brady was worried about Sue. She wasn't exactly used to being outdoors. She knew her way around a hot stove or a wash pot as well as anybody, but as far as he knew, she'd never spent a lot of time on top of a horse. But there wasn't anything he could do about that.

"What happens to them is their look out," he said. "I'm sorry they didn't wait for the marshal and me to do something, but now that they're out here, they'll have to take care of themselves."

"What if they run across them outlaws?" Harry asked. "I don't doubt Miss Ellie can take care of herself, but I don't know if Miz Tolbert knows one end of a gun from the other."

Brady was pretty sure she didn't. Sue was probably a whole lot less expert at shooting than she was at riding, unless Lane had spent some time teaching her, and there was no reason to think that he would have. Why would she need to know about shooting? And even if Lane had taken her out a time or two and let her shoot at some target like a prickly pear, something like that most likely wouldn't help her if she met up with Angel. There was a lot of difference between shooting at a cactus and shooting at your own brother, especially if he was shooting back at you.

And Brady was pretty sure that Angel would probably just as soon shoot his sister as to bust up a horse turd. Which was another reason there wasn't going to be any turning back.

They were crossing a wide clear area, of which there were plenty around Blanco, when they saw the rain coming toward them like a gray curtain.

"Better get out your slickers, boys," Moon said. He scratched his bristly beard. We're about to get a soakin'. This'll get that old river on the rise."

Brady unrolled his slicker and slipped it over his head. "What about that river? How far is it from here?"

"Few miles," Willis said. Always able to see the bad side of things, he added, "We'd best not have to cross it, considerin' the direction that rain's comin' from. It'll be runnin' fast and deep. Drown ever' damn one of us."

"Angel's prob'ly already crossed," Shag said. "Prob'ly be long gone before we can ever get to the other side."

"We'll find a way to get across," Brady said. "One way or the other."

"I wouldn't bet on that," Shag said. "You ain't never seen that river when it's runnin' high and wide."

"I'll see it now, then, " Brady told him. "Let's go."

The rain swept over them as they moved on.

Chapter 24

—◄✖►—

Ellie was wearing an old hat that had belonged to her husband, Burt. She wore it now and then when she was out in the sun, but it wasn't sunny now. Water ran off the brim and fell in a stream in front of her face. She hunched into the slicker and asked Sue how she was doing. She had to speak up to be heard over the sound of the rain.

"Fine," Sue said.

She, too, had on a slicker, and a wide-brimmed hat covered her yellow hair.

"This rain's going to make the river rise," Ellie said. "And that's the way Angel was heading."

"Do you think he's already across?"

"I'd guess that he is. He got a good start on us."

"Is there any way we can catch him?"

Ellie was feeling hollow inside again, the way she had when the trouble had started.

"I don't know."

"But you're not going to turn back, are you?"

"No. You can if you want to. I wouldn't blame you."

"I'm not sure I could find the way even if I wanted to," Sue said. "But I'm not going back if you don't." She paused. "You don't think they'd try to cross the river if it was in flood, do you?"

Ellie knew that the level of the river could change alarmingly when there was a hard rain. She didn't know Angel, but she didn't think anyone would be foolish enough to attempt a crossing at the wrong time. On the other hand, he might get caught off guard. It had happened to more than one person.

She didn't want to say that to Sue. So she said, "If he was going to cross, he'd have done it already. We'll just have to see what it's like, and if it's too high and fast, we'll wait till it goes down."

"How long will that take?"

"I don't know. But I'm not going to quit."

"I didn't think you were. But we're going to be mighty uncomfortable."

"I'm not worried about that," Ellie said. She'd been uncomfortable before. "Maybe we can find us a place to wait that's out of the rain. There used to be a little church not too far from here. It hasn't been used in a long time, but it'll probably keep the rain off us."

"Can you find it?"

"I think so," Ellie said, though she wasn't really sure. "If we're lucky, we can get there before we get too wet."

* * *

"This damn wind is blowing rain up under my slicker," Shag said. "We need to find us some place to hole up till it's over with."

Brady looked out through the rain. All he could see was the dark gray outline of some of the hills in the distance.

"You got any place in mind?" he asked.

"Used to be an old church around in here somewhere, down near the river. If it's still standin', we could at least get under a roof."

Brady didn't like the idea of taking shelter for any length of time. He wanted to stay after Angel, though he had to admit that they'd lost the trail almost as soon as the rain started. It was dark, and the rain was washing out any signs that someone might have left behind.

"Did Miss Taine know about the church?" he asked.

"Might've," Shag said. "She's lived around here all her life. Why?"

"If she knew about it, she might try to get out of the rain there."

"She might at that," Shag agreed. "She's a right smart woman."

"We'll give it a look, then," Brady told him. "If you can find it, that is."

"I can find it," Shag said. "Don't worry yourself about that."

* * *

The rain drummed against what was left of the roof of the old church building and poured in through the holes, washing away part of one of the bird nests. It blew in through the windows in sheets.

Laurie sat in the corner, well away from Hoot, and watched the water coming in and running across the floor. She was cold and uncomfortable, and she had decided she wasn't going to stay with her uncle Angel any longer than she had to.

He'd lied to her about the picnic. There wasn't anything to eat except some old dried biscuits, some syrup to put on them, and some cold tomatoes out of a can. The only good thing was the canned peaches for dessert, but the peaches didn't make up for the rest.

Besides, Uncle Angel had lied to her about other things. She was sure her mother and father wouldn't want her to be out here in the rain with him, no matter what he told her. She'd been looking around at the countryside as they rode, and she thought she could find her way back home by herself if she had to. But maybe she wouldn't have to. Maybe Angel would take her if she asked him.

"When are we going back to Miss Ellie's ranch?" she said.

Angel looked over at her from where he was lying stretched out on the floor with his head resting on his saddle. His booted feet were only a few inches from a puddle of rainwater, but he didn't seem to notice.

"Well, now, I can't rightly answer that," he said. "I don't know when this rain is likely to stop."

"When it stops, will we leave?" Laurie asked.

"I can't say for sure," Angel told her. "You never know what we might do next."

Laurie took that to mean that Angel knew very well what he was going to do, but whatever it was, he wasn't going to tell her. That made her all the more determined to leave.

She wished she had on some real clothes instead of just her nightgown, and most of all she wished she had a pair of shoes. But her feet were tough. She went barefoot most of the year around the house. She could walk a long way without shoes if she had to.

She wondered if she could ride a mule all by herself. She was pretty sure she could, but the men had taken the saddles when they hobbled the mules. She couldn't ride without a saddle and bridle. Well, she'd just have to walk, and that was that.

Of course, Uncle Angel wasn't going to let her just walk away. She knew that. For some reason he wanted her with him, but she didn't care what he wanted. She was going to leave anyway.

The others would be watching her, too, so she'd have to be careful, especially of Mr. Hoot. She still didn't like the way he looked at her, and she didn't like the way his voice sounded when he talked to her. It sounded different from when he was talking to the others.

Laurie thought that Mr. Jephson would let her go if

he had anything to say about it, but Uncle Angel was the boss, and he wasn't going to let Mr. Jephson have a say.

She looked at the window. The rain was still coming down, maybe even harder than it had earlier, though the wind didn't seem to be blowing quite so much. Laurie couldn't leave while it was raining like that. She'd have to wait until it stopped or at least slowed down some. When it did, she'd slip away. She didn't know exactly how she'd do it, but she would. Somehow.

Chapter 25

Angel relaxed and closed his eyes and listened to the sound of the rain. He could have told Laurie the truth, which was that he had no plans to go anywhere, but it wasn't any of her business. He was quite content to wait in the ruined church. He knew they'd come to him, sooner or later.

That was the secret he hadn't told Jephson. He hadn't told Hoot, either. He hadn't told anyone. It was all a part of his plan, the one that had come into his head not long after he'd taken care of Rankin and Hob Bowman. He was going to take care of everyone who'd put him into prison.

He'd been disappointed when he discovered that his sister had moved from Fort Worth, but he'd gotten over that when he found out where she was living. He could still make the plan work. In fact, it might work out even better. He knew the country around Blanco, and he remembered the old church. It wasn't an especially good place for what he had in mind, but it would have to do.

He was a little worried about Jephson and Hoot,

though. Angel opened his eyes and saw that Hoot was sitting with his back to the wall, whittling on a stick that he'd picked up off the floor, cutting a glance at Laurie now and then when he thought Angel wasn't looking at him.

Hoot was a good man to have on your side in a fight, no doubt about it, but he was a little peculiar. There was something twisted in him, something that even Angel, who knew about twisted insides, couldn't put a finger on. Hoot had done his part at the ranch, though, and Angel thought he could trust him in a tight spot.

Jephson was a different story. There was something about Jephson that bothered Angel quite a bit. Jephson didn't seem to have the nerve for killing. He looked like a killer, and plenty of men in the prison had been scared of him, but he didn't *act* like a killer. He acted like someone who'd be more at home walking behind a plow or branding a calf.

So Angel would have to keep an eye on Hoot and Jephson both, though he didn't think that either of them would cause any immediate trouble. There was no way they were going to try anything with the weather acting up like it was. This wasn't just some fast-moving thunderstorm like the one they'd been in on the day of their escape. This was the kind of rain that was going to last for a while.

Angel thought about his plan. He wondered if Lane was dead. He hoped not, but he couldn't be sure. It had been so dark in the house that he could hardly see, and he'd been in too much of a hurry to check on Lane. He'd wanted to get his hands on Laurie and get out of there before anyone could stop him.

It was too bad that Lane had shot Abilene Jack. Jack was the only one that Angel had trusted. He was the kind of man who'd do what was necessary and not have any second thoughts about it.

Angel figured that Abilene Jack was dead for sure. That shotgun blast was just about guaranteed to finish him off, and Lane had already shot him once.

Angel wasn't surprised that Lane had been able to put a bullet into Jack, but the shotgun was completely unexpected. Angel had told Hoot and Jephson to watch the bunkhouse and make sure that no one came out, but he hadn't thought anything about the main house. There hadn't been anyone in there except those two women, not that Angel had seen, and he hadn't thought there'd be any trouble from them. Well, it was just Abilene Jack's bad luck that one of the women had a little sand in her craw. Angel never mourned for anyone.

He closed his eyes again and wondered who'd show up at the little abandoned church. Lane would, if he was able. Sue, maybe. But the one he was really counting on was Brady Tolbert. Sue and Lane were the ones who'd turned on their own kin, which was bad enough, but Brady was the one who'd come for him and taken him to jail. The way Angel saw it, Brady was the one most directly responsible for putting Angel behind the walls at Huntsville for more than two years. And he would've been there much longer if he hadn't gotten lucky.

And Angel could still remember Brady's last words to him as the cell door was swinging shut after Brady had brought him in. Brady had stared at Angel, his eyes hard, and said, "If you ever mess with my family again, I won't bring you back here. I'll kill you myself."

And then the son of a bitch had smiled. So Angel hoped that they managed to get word to Brady about what had happened. It would take him a few days to get there, most likely, but he'd come a-running when he found out that his brother had been shot and his niece had been stolen away.

That was why Angel had taken Laurie, of course. He didn't care about the girl, but he knew that if she was with him, they'd come after him. All of them if they could, but some of them for sure.

He could've killed Lane and Sue in their beds, and he'd even considered it. But that would've been too easy on Lane and Sue. They wouldn't know that he'd taken their daughter, and they'd suffer a lot more if they were wondering what he was going to do with Laurie, which was why he was hoping Abilene Jack hadn't killed Lane when he'd shot him.

Let them suffer, Angel thought. That was what he wanted them to do. It served them right. They had no way of knowing that Angel really cared about Laurie, in a way that he couldn't quite explain. He'd never do anything to hurt her, and he wouldn't let anyone else hurt her, not if he could help it. He didn't mind at all hurting the people she loved, but Laurie was different.

When she'd been not much more than a baby she'd told him she loved him. As far back as Angel could remember, no one had ever told him that before, not and really meant it. He planned to take care of her as best he could. Maybe when all this was over, they could go down and live in Mexico. He'd tell people that she was his little girl. With her hair looking almost as blond as his, people down there were likely to believe him.

Angel smiled thinking about it. He'd heard the law in Mexico wasn't near as hard to deal with as it was in Texas. He could have a good life across the Rio Grande.

He heard a noise and opened his eyes. Jephson was walking around like a jittery cat, trying to avoid the water that was coming in through the roof.

"I've heard tell that rivers out here can flood quicker than a cat can wink its eye," Jephson said. "You reckon we're far enough off to be safe?"

Hoot stopped whittling. "How long's this church been here? It ain't been carried off yet."

"He's right," Angel said, sitting up. "There's no danger up this far."

He wished Jephson wouldn't act so high-strung. That was another thing that bothered Angel. Hoot was steady as a stone when things got a little dicey, but Jephson always got wrought up and anxious.

Angel was more like Hoot. He didn't worry about things he couldn't control. He did tend to fret a little about things like how much ammunition and how many guns they had, but he thought that was pretty well taken care of.

They had the sawed-off shotgun they'd taken from Rankin, and while it didn't have much range, it would do just fine for close-in work. Angel had managed to get a Colt's Peacemaker for himself, and Hoot had one, too. Jephson had an old Colt's Navy that had been worked over to take cartridges. It would've been better if they'd had a rifle, but they didn't. That was too bad, but they'd just have to make the best of it.

It would have been better, too, if the walls of the church had been three or four feet thick instead of being made of boards worn so thin that you could practically stick your finger through them. But at least they offered some protection even if it wasn't much.

It would have to do, because Angel wasn't going anywhere. He was going to stay right where he was and wait till someone came.

He hoped it would be Lane, if Lane was still alive.

He hoped even more that it would be Brady, though that might mean they'd have to stay in the church for a couple of days. After they'd all worried themselves sick about Laurie, Angel could kill them knowing that he'd done the worst he could do. He hoped they could hole up in the church till Brady got there and that Jephson wouldn't lose his nerve.

Angel would have to do something about Laurie when the shooting started. He hadn't quite decided about that. He couldn't just let her go. That would mean he couldn't take her to Mexico with him later on.

And he was sure there'd be a later on. It never entered his head that he might not survive whatever fight ensued. There were going to be some people killed, he didn't have any doubt about that, but he didn't plan to be one of them.

And neither would Laurie. After that, well, to tell the truth, Angel just didn't care.

Chapter 26

"Somebody's comin'," Hoot said. "I can hear 'em out there."

It was late afternoon, nearly nightfall, and it was quite dark both outside and inside the church. Angel couldn't hear a thing except the pounding of the rain, but he didn't doubt Hoot, who could hear things no one else could. Maybe it was those jug ears of his.

"All right," Angel said. "See if you can get a look at 'em."

Hoot went to a window. "Can't see a thing. Too dark and rainy. They're out there, though."

Angel went to the church's front door. He didn't have to open it. There was a large crack between the door and the frame, plenty of space for him to peep out. He thought he saw two figures on horseback, but he couldn't be sure.

"Can't tell too much," he said. But we'd best be ready."

He took out the Colt and checked the cylinder.

"Who gets the shotgun?" Hoot asked.

"We won't need that for a while," Angel said. "You ready, Jephson?"

Jephson didn't look ready. He looked to Angel like a man who wished he were somewhere else. But he said, "I'm ready as I'll ever be."

"Good," Angel said. He walked over to where Laurie was sitting, reached down, and picked her up. "Time for you to go somewhere else."

"I don't want to go anywhere," Laurie said, but Angel paid her no mind.

"I'm gonna stash you in the back room for a little while. You be a good girl and I'll come for you later."

There was a small room not far from where the altar had once been. Maybe the preachers who came there needed a private place for some reason or other. Angel didn't know what preachers did, and he didn't care. All he knew was that the room was a good place to put Laurie, well out of the way of whatever was going to happen.

He set her on the floor and went out, closing the door behind him. There was no lock on the door, not even a handle, but Angel picked up a small limb that had come in through the roof and jammed it under the bottom of the door so that Laurie couldn't shove it open.

Laurie pounded on the other side of the door with her fists and called out to Angel, who said, "Keep quiet in there. Those folks out there might be outlaws comin' to look for a dry place. I don't want them to find you."

The pounding stopped.

"Hell," Hoot said, "I though *we* were the outlaws."

Angel drew his Peacemaker and leveled it at Hoot. "You'll be a dead son of a bitch if she hears you say anything like that."

"I forgot," Hoot said.

"Don't forget again. What's going on outside?"

"I don't know. There's still someone ridin' around out there, though."

"Why don't they try to come in, then?"

"Don't ask me. Maybe they know we're in here."

"There's no way they could know that," Angel said. He looked over at Jephson. "What do you think?"

"I don't know what to think," Jephson said. Except that we should've kept on going."

Angel smiled. "Too late for that now."

Ellie sat on her horse and looked at the old church building. It was dark inside and out. It seemed to her that it might fall down at any moment under the weight of the rain or topple over to one side, pushed by the wind.

Ellie wiped water out of her eyes and said to Sue, "Not much of a shelter."

"It's better than nothing," Sue said. "Let's get inside."

"Not yet," Ellie said.

She had a bad feeling about the place, and she knew better than to go into a place she hadn't studied for a while. You never knew what you might run into, especially when you were on the trail of a man like Angel Ware.

"Do you know much about using that pistol of Lane's you brought with you?" Ellie asked.

"Lane taught me," Sue said. "I know enough."

Ellie hoped she was right. "Let's ride around to the back," she said. "Look the place over."

Hoot was looking out the window, his eyes just above the level of the sill.

"They're goin' around back," he said. "They'll see the mules."

Angel didn't want that to happen, not before he knew who it was. It might be Lane. Hell, it might even be Brady. He would have liked for things to have worked out a little differently. He wanted them to know he had Laurie. He wanted them to know it was him that was killing them. But it didn't seem as if things were going to work out that way. It was too bad, but there was nothing to be done about it.

"Stop 'em," he said.

Hoot stood up and started firing his pistol. Flame streaked from the barrel, and smoke swirled around Hoot's head. The sound of the shots was deafening in the small confines of the old building.

Ellie's horse was picking its way through the cemetery. The first shot missed Ellie by inches, and her horse bolted forward through the rain. Sue's horse reared up, throwing Sue to the ground. Her head struck one of the tombstones, and she lay there without moving, the rain streaming over her face.

"Did you hear that noise?" Harry Moon said. "Sounded like gunshots to me."

Brady wasn't sure. The rain muffled sound, and it could have been just distant thunder. On the other hand, it might have been gunshots.

"Where's it coming from?" he asked.

"Sounds like it might be comin' from that church I was tellin' you about," Shag said. "Maybe we oughta stay away from there. No tellin' what we might be ridin' into."

"Might be those killers we're after," Fred Willis said, always looking on the dark side. "Might be they're shootin' at Miss Ellie."

"If I know Miss Ellie, more likely she's shootin' at them," Moon said.

It didn't matter to Brady who was doing the shooting. One thing was for sure, Laurie wasn't doing any shooting, and if she was anywhere around, she was in danger. So were Ellie Taine and Sue.

"We'd better get ourselves over there," he said. "See what's happening. Maybe we'll get this over with right now."

"Best idea I've heard all day," Moon said. He mashed his dilapidated hat down on his head. "Lead the way, Shag."

Tillman reluctantly took the lead, and the others followed close behind.

Chapter 27

When Laurie heard the shots, she knew what she was going to do. She was going to get out of there.

There was a little window with no glass in it, but it was up higher than she could reach. If only she had a chair to stand on, she might be able to get her hands on the sill and climb out, but there was no chair in the room. There was nothing at all.

Laurie walked over and stood directly under the window. She stretched out on tiptoe and reached up. The sill was still several inches away.

More shots were fired, but Laurie hardly heard them. She was concentrating on the window. A gust of rain came through and wet her face. She wiped her eyes, crouched down, and jumped straight up.

Her fingers gripped the sill for a second, but the sill was wet, and her fingers slipped off. Laurie dropped back to the floor.

She didn't waste time feeling sorry that she'd failed.

She jumped again. This time, she got hold. She hung still for a moment, then began pulling herself up, kicking her bare feet against the wall.

In seconds, she was balanced on the windowsill. She knew that it was a long way to the ground, and she couldn't see much at all. It was too dark, and the rain got in her eyes. But she wasn't going to stay in the church, not with all the shooting going on.

She was about to jump when Angel came crashing into the room, throwing the door hard against the wall behind him.

"You hold on a minute there," he said.

Laurie didn't listen to him. She jumped.

She hit the ground hard, but the ground itself was soft mud, and she splattered water and mud everywhere.

I've ruined my gown, she thought. The rain plastered her hair to her face, and she pushed it back out of the way. It didn't help much. She could see hardly anything.

Now what do I do? she wondered.

Ellie owned a Navy Colt that had belonged to her husband, but she'd brought Jonathan Crossland's Peacemaker instead. As soon as she managed to get her horse stopped, she drew the pistol. She didn't fire it, however. She was afraid that Laurie might be in the church.

She looked around for Sue, but she couldn't see her. Then she saw Sue's horse, with its empty saddle.

First Lane, now Sue, she thought. The hollow feeling she'd had for so long began to be replaced by a burning sensation that Ellie remembered all too well. It was easy enough to tell yourself that you'd changed, that you'd learned the uselessness of revenge, but when you were faced with people who were trying to kill folks you cared about, telling yourself didn't count for much.

Ellie made sure to keep some of the big trees between herself and the church. She kept a watch on the window that the shots had come from. Laurie wouldn't be near the window. No matter how bad her uncle was, he wouldn't put her in the way of a bullet. No one would do that. Or at least Ellie hoped no one would.

She steadied her arm and squeezed off two shots through the window.

For a second there was no reaction. Then there were two answering shots, and a bullet thwacked into the tree in front of Ellie.

She fired again, and someone inside the church yelled. Good. Maybe she got one of them. That would leave two. They'd probably stay away from the window for a while.

She calmly replaced the three cartridges that she'd fired and tried to think of what to do next.

Laurie heard the shots from the trees. She didn't know who was doing the shooting, but she knew that whoever it was must not be a friend of Angel's. She decided to find out who it was before Angel came after her. She started to walk as fast as she could toward the trees.

The mud sucked at her feet, and the rain was very cold.

"The kid got away," Angel said. "I'm goin' after her."

Hoot was sitting on the floor by the window. There was blood all over his shirt, and blood was still dripping from what remained of his left earlobe.

"Somebody shot off my ear," he said. "I'm gonna bleed to death."

"You've still got most of your ear," Angel said. "It's nothing to worry about. Ears just bleed a lot. Stay clear of the window, and you'll be all right."

"What if you don't come back?"

"Then you're on your own," Angel told him, heading for the back door.

When Angel had left the building, Jephson said, "We don't have to stay here either. We can just get on those mules and leave."

Hoot looked thoughtful. "Where would we go?"

Jephson couldn't answer that one. He didn't know the country, and the weather wasn't improving any.

"Well?" Hoot said.

"I don't know."

"What I thought. So we might as well stay in here where it's dry."

Jephson didn't think that was such a good idea. He thought that getting out of that church would be the smart thing to do, wet or not, even if they didn't know where they were. But he wasn't going alone.

He shrugged. "I guess we stay, then."

Hoot touched his earlobe, looked at his bloody fingertips, and said, "Yeah. Besides, we got more company comin'."

"How can you tell?"

"I still got enough of an ear left to hear with," Hoot said.

Brady Tolbert looked at the dilapidated building and wondered if there was really anyone inside. After the first few gunshots, if that's what they were, there hadn't been any further commotion.

"What do you think?" Shag Tillman asked.

"I think we wait here for a little bit," Brady said. Like Ellie, he knew better than to hurry into any place that might prove to be dangerous. "I don't like to rush things."

"Can't blame you for that," Moon said. "But it's mighty wet out here."

"Better to be a little wet than a whole lot dead," Willis said. "We don't know but what those killers are in there waitin' for us."

"If they are, why ain't they shootin'?" Moon said. "Maybe our ears was playin' tricks on us."

Brady caught movement out of the corner of his eye. He looked toward the trees and saw a dark smudge of motion. Someone yelled, "Miss Ellie! Miss Ellie!"

And then the shooting started again.

Chapter 28

—◆—✦◆✦—◆—

Angel saw Laurie running toward someone on horseback in the trees. When Laurie began shouting "Miss Ellie," Angel fired three rapid shots at the rider.

He missed, and Ellie fired back. But being taken by surprise as she was, and not being an expert marksman in the first place she didn't hit her mark.

Nor did Angel. He was running through the dark in the rain while he fired, and he would have been extremely lucky to hit anything under those conditions.

Laurie, frightened by the shooting, tripped over a fallen limb and fell into the mud. She lay still, hoping that none of the bullets would come her way.

When the shooting broke out, Brady Tolbert drew his pistol and turned his horse's head in the direction of the muzzle flashes. Just then the front door of the church burst open. A man stood just inside the doorway, blasting away with his revolver.

Brady heard Fred Willis grunt and saw him slip sideways out of the saddle. Harry Moon turned toward Fred as if to catch him before he fell, and a bullet gouged a chunk of flesh out of Harry's side, splattering Brady with Moon's blood.

Harry moaned aloud but stayed in the saddle, bent over the horn. Willis lay on the ground and didn't move.

Brady began firing into the open doorway, but the door slammed shut. The bullets ripped through the wood, but Brady knew no one was standing in their way. He stopped shooting and looked around for the marshal. Tillman was nowhere to be seen. Brady was disappointed, though he wasn't surprised.

The Ranger thumbed cartridges into the chambers of his revolver as he tried to decide what to do next.

Charge the church and try to get inside?

Find out what the shooting was about out there in the trees?

He thought the shouts he'd heard might have come from a young girl, which meant that Laurie could be there in the darkness. He headed in that direction.

Ellie dismounted and started toward where she thought she'd heard Laurie's voice. She had to be careful, because someone besides Laurie, probably Angel, was also out there. She wished the clouds would part and let some moonlight through, but she knew that wasn't going to happen.

She went cautiously from tree to tree, not wanting to

give Angel another shot at her if she could help it, although she knew he could see no better than she could.

She wanted to call Laurie's name, to let her know that someone was there looking for her, but she didn't dare. If she said a word, she'd give away her location and give Angel a direction in which to shoot. Besides, Laurie knew Ellie was there. Her young eyes were better in the darkness than Ellie's were, and she'd seen Ellie on her horse.

"Miss Ellie! Where are you?"

Laurie was calling her from somewhere just ahead. Ellie stopped to listen. She could hear the rain rattling through the leaves and the wind whipping the branches over her head, but that was all.

Then shooting broke out from inside the church and from in front of it. Gunshots thundered so fast that Ellie couldn't count them. Hoping that Angel was as distracted as she was, she risked calling out Laurie's name.

"I'm here, Miss Ellie!" came the response. "I'm over here!"

Ellie turned slightly to her right and started forward. She had taken only one step when she heard Laurie again.

"No! I don't want to go with you! No! No!"

Laurie's voice was cut off after the final "No!" Ellie stopped being cautious and ran forward.

Brady was in the middle of the little cemetery when someone started shooting at him from the church again. He fired back at the open window, but he was pretty sure he wasn't hitting anyone.

He slid off his horse and took cover behind one of the upright tombstones. The men in the church couldn't see him any better than he could see them, so he felt relatively safe. He'd wait until they risked another shot, then fire at the flash.

It was a good plan, except that there wasn't another flash. He waited for several minutes, then stood up. He heard nothing other than the wind and the rain. He started to lead his horse among the tombstones and almost stepped on someone lying on the ground in front of him.

Hoot and Jephson saddled the mules as best they could in the circumstances. Jephson had convinced Hoot that it was time to vacate the premises and leave Angel behind. After all, Angel had told them that if he didn't come back, they were on their own.

Jephson didn't like the idea of leaving Angel much better than Hoot did. He wasn't at all sure they could manage without Angel, but he couldn't think of any alternatives other than staying in the church and getting killed.

Hoot probably would've enjoyed that, Jephson thought. When he'd thrown open that door and started shooting, he was laughing like a drunk man, and if Jephson hadn't pulled him back and slammed the door, he would probably have just stood there until someone shot him to pieces. He'd started shooting out the window again, but Jephson had stopped him and finally persuaded him that it was time to take off.

They had the mules almost ready when Angel showed up. He was carrying the girl under one arm.

"Runnin' out on me, are you?" Angel said.

"You told us we were on our own," Jephson said. "Remember?"

"I killed two of the bastards, Angel," Hoot said. He was holding the sawed-off shotgun by his side. "Maybe three." He looked at Laurie. "Is the girl dead?"

He sounded disappointed to Jephson, who figured the girl was better off dead than in Hoot's charge.

"She's not dead," Angel said. "I had to hit her, as much as I hated it. She was tryin' to get away."

"Imagine that," Jephson said. "She must not like our company."

"I don't like a smart mouth," Angel said. "Saddle one of those mules for me."

Hoot handed the shotgun to Jephson and dashed back into the church and brought out a saddle and bridle. He tossed the saddle to Jephson, who caught it by the horn with his free hand. Jephson handed the shotgun back to Hoot and threw the saddle on the mule's back.

"Cinch 'er up tight," Angel said.

"Don't bother," Ellie said, stepping out from behind a tree.

She was holding her Peacemaker level with both hands, pointing it straight at Angel.

Brady knelt down and looked in the face of his sister-in-law, who wasn't looking back.

"Sue," he said, reaching down a hand to touch her.

Her face was cold and wet with rain. His hand touched her neck. He could feel a pulse, faint but definite, and he began looking for a wound. There was none that he could see, but he could feel a stickiness in the hair on the back of her head where it had hit the tombstone. He needed to get her inside, out of the rain, where she could get warm and dry.

He picked her up. She was a substantial woman, but he could carry her. He didn't know what he would do when he got to the church, however. He was certain that whoever was inside wasn't going to welcome him.

He didn't care. He'd worry about that when he got there.

Shag Tillman was thoroughly ashamed of himself. He'd run off when the shooting started, just wheeled his horse around and turned tail. He'd always known he wasn't the bravest man in Blanco, but he'd never really thought he'd show himself to be a flat-footed coward when it came right down to it.

He had, though, and he might as well admit it, hard

as that was for him to do. When the shooting started, he'd proved out to be yellow as snot.

The question was, what could he do about it?

He supposed he could ride on back to town. If everyone was dead back at the church, there wouldn't be anyone to say what he'd done.

But what if some of them were still alive, as they were likely to be, no thanks to him? If they were, they wouldn't be thinking too highly of Shag Tillman right about now.

That was what finally decided him. The idea of people thinking he was yellower than a cur dog proved to be even more painful to him than the thought of what might happen to him if he rode back to the church. He had to prove to them and to himself that he wasn't as bad as they thought. That he wasn't as bad as *he* thought.

He turned his horse around.

Brady was surprised when he heard someone calling out his name.

"Mr. Tolbert? Who's that you're carryin?"

It was Tillman, the marshal. Brady thought he'd seen the last of him, at least for the time being.

"It's my sister-in-law," he said. "She's hurt."

"You gonna take her in the church?"

"Don't see any other place around here to take her," Brady said.

"Might be dangerous."

"Can't help that."

Shag slid off his horse. "I'll go in first."

"You don't have to do that," Brady told him.

"Yessir, I do," Shag said.

He slopped through the mud, pistol in hand. When he got to the church, he mounted the little stoop, drew back his leg, and kicked in the door. It whined back on its hinges and hit the wall.

"All right, you sons of bitches," Shag said. "Here I am."

There was no answer from inside, and after pausing for a second, Shag stepped into the darkness.

"You can come on in now," he called to Brady. "I think I musta scared 'em off."

Brady could hear the relief in the marshal's voice.

"I'm sure you did," he said.

Chapter 29

— ⊷≡⊶ —

There was noise in the church, so Ellie knew that someone was in there. But she didn't know who it was. She hoped it wasn't some friend of Angel.

"Just put the girl down," she said, "and I won't shoot."

"Hell, you can shoot if you want to," Angel told her. "Hoot here, he'd have that shotgun turned on you before I hit the ground." He gave Ellie a cagey look. "Or maybe he'd just shoot the girl."

Ellie didn't know what to say to that, and she saw that the man Angel had called Hoot was bringing the shotgun up slowly so that both barrels were pointed at her. And he was smiling as if shooting her would be the most amusing thing he could think of doing right then.

"You must be the lady that killed Abilene Jack," Angel continued. "I wish you hadn't done that, but I guess I can't hold it against you."

"That's right kind of you," Ellie said.

"My sister come with you?" Angel asked.

Ellie wasn't sure how to answer. Finally she said, "Yes."

"So she knows I have Laurie?"

"She knows."

"Where is she now?"

"I think you killed her."

"If she's killed, it wasn't me that did it. It was Hoot. He likes shooting folks. Ain't that right, Hoot?"

Hoot didn't say anything. He just kept right on smiling and pointing the shotgun at Laurie.

"Wish it had been me that killed her, though," Angel said. "Would've served her right for what she did to me. She's the one that got me sent to prison."

"Killing people doesn't change anything," Ellie said, though she'd thought it did at one time.

"That's your opinion, I guess." Angel said. "And you're welcome to it. How about Lane? He dead too?"

"No. You didn't kill him."

"It wasn't me that tried to. It was Abilene Jack. Too bad he didn't finish the job. Maybe I'll get the chance later on. But that don't have much to do with where we are right now. And right now, looks like we have ourselves a little standoff here. So I'm gonna be movin' along. I don't think you want Hoot to kill the girl, which is what he'll do if you try to shoot me. Cinch up that saddle for me, Ben."

Jephson tightened the cinch, and Angel climbed onto the mule, still holding Laurie's inert form. Hoot switched the shotgun from Laurie to Ellie.

Angel laid Laurie across his lap and said, "I'll be leavin' the three of you now. See you boys on down the road, assumin' you get there. And, lady?"

"What?" Ellie said.

"The main reason I'm not tellin' Hoot to shoot you right now is that I want you to deliver a message for me. If you happen to see a fella name of Brady Tolbert along the trail, tell him I'll be lookin' out for him."

I'll tell him. If I see him."

"I figgered you would," Angel said.

He rode off into the rain, with Jephson looking after him and Hoot still standing there with the shotgun.

Ellie was almost overwhelmed by her rage, at both Angel and herself. At Angel because he'd read her correctly, and at herself because she hadn't tried to kill him anyway.

"I don't know who you are lady," Hoot said to her, still smiling. "I don't even give a damn about you killin' Abilene Jack, though we celled together up at Huntsville. But all the same, I'd just as soon kill you as not."

"Forget it, kid," Jephson said. "Angel wants her to deliver a message for him, remember? What we're gonna do is leave here right now, and I don't think this lady's gonna try to stop us. Are up?"

"No," Ellie said. "I won't try to stop you."

"Fine with me," Hoot said. "Why don't you head on out, Ben. "I'll just wait till you're out of range of that six-shooter the lady's holdin'."

Jephson got on the mule and rode off. When his dark form had faded into the trees, Hoot said to Ellie, "I could pull this trigger right now and cut you half in two."

"I know you could try," Ellie told him. "But I've still got this pistol. Maybe I'd get you first."

"You might at that. But I don't think you will."

Hoot turned away from her, put his foot in the stirrup, and swung up on the mule. Then he turned back to Ellie and raised his hand.

"Maybe I'll see you again," he said.

"I hope so," Ellie said, but she didn't mean it in a friendly way.

Hoot knew that, and he laughed. Ellie watched him ride away, knowing that it would do no good at all to kill him. She didn't have anything particular against back-shooting, but she didn't want to give Angel any excuse to harm Laurie, which he might decide to do if she killed his friend.

She stood there for a moment and let the rain run off her hat and then turned to go into the church.

Shag Tillman opened the back door before she got there and said, "Is that you, Miss Ellie?"

That was just like Shag Tillman, Ellie thought. Showing up right after the last chance for him to do anything had already passed by. Not that he would have done anything even if he'd shown up sooner. He didn't have any more of a backbone than one of those night crawlers she'd used for catfish bait when she was a little girl.

"It's me, Shag," she said. "You're a day late and a dollar short again."

"We got a lot of trouble in here, Miss Ellie," he said. "We got Sue Tolbert and Fred Willis and Harry Moon all laid out in the floor, and one of 'em's dead."

Ellie was sure that Sue was the dead one, but she asked, "Which one?"

"It's Fred. Those sons of bitches shot him and Harry without any warnin'. Pardon my language."

Ellie didn't care about his language. "But Sue's still alive?"

"Sure is. Got a big bump on the back of her head, though. And Harry, well, he's shot up pretty bad, but he's still breathin'."

Ellie pushed past Shag and went into the church. Water dripped off her slicker and pooled on the floor. It was too dark to see much at all, but she could make out the three dark figures lying near the front door. And there was someone kneeling next to them.

"Who's that?" Ellie asked.

"Texas Ranger name of Brady Tolbert," Shag said. "He's Lane Tolbert's brother."

"I've heard about him," Ellie said.

"He found Miz Tolbert out there in the cemetery," Shag went on. "We thought she was shot at first, but maybe she just fell off her horse and hit her head."

"I need to talk to her," Ellie said. "Is she awake?"

"I don't know about that. She wasn't when I went to

the door. Was you talkin' to somebody out there? I thought I heard somethin', but I couldn't be sure, what with all the noise the rain's makin'.' "

Shag was right about the rain. It was pounding against the church as if it were about to come right through the walls. And some of it was streaming through holes in the roof.

"Sue's brother was out there," Ellie said. "And two other men. The ones who came to my ranch last night. They had Laurie."

"I guess that's why you let 'em leave."

"That's why. They might've killed her if I hadn't."

"They're mean'uns, sure enough."

"I have to tell Sue about her daughter."

"Go ahead," Shag said. I don't know that she can hear you, though."

Ellie walked across the church, dripping water every step of the way. Brady Tolbert looked up when she neared him. Ellie couldn't see him very well in the darkness, but she thought that he favored his brother, except that his face was a little more lined, his eyes a little narrower, and his mouth a little harder.

"I'm Ellie Taine," she said.

"I thought you might be," he said. "I guess the marshal told you that I'm Brady Tolbert."

"He told me. Angel wants you to know that he'll be looking out for you."

The hard mouth smiled. It didn't soften any when it did.

"That sounds like Angel," Brady said. "Does he still have Laurie?"

"He does. I wanted to let Sue know that, and that Laurie's all right."

Ellie had decided not to mention that Angel had knocked Laurie out. She didn't want Sue to worry. Ellie was already worried enough for both of them.

"Ellie?"

It was Sue's voice, faint but steady.

"I'm here," Ellie said.

"I heard what you said. Thank God Laurie's all right."

"I don't think Angel will hurt her," Ellie said, knowing that he already had.

"I know he wouldn't. He may not be worth much, but he wouldn't hurt my girl." She paused, then continued. "Even if he wouldn't, we still have to get her back."

"You let me worry about that," Ellie said. "You just rest and get better."

"There's not much else she can do," Brady said.

"What about Mr. Moon?" Ellie asked.

"He's hurt bad. Got a big chunk shot out of his side, but the marshal and I got it cleaned up as best as we could. Not much we could do for the other man, though."

Ellie thought for a moment about Fred Willis. He'd never complained about one thing he had to do on the ranch. She remembered once when a calf had kicked him at branding time. He'd had a knot on his shin as big as a cat's head, but it never slowed him down.

"He was a good man," she said.

"I'm sure he was."

"I'm going after Angel," Ellie said. "He's not going to get away."

"Someone has to stay here and take care of these folks," Brady told her. "And someone should go for help. Moon's not going to be able to ride. He'll have to be put in a wagon and carried back to town."

"I can give Mr. Moon any help he needs until help gets here," Sue said. "I'll be fine. The marshal can ride into town and get a wagon."

That was a good job for Shag, Ellie thought. She surely didn't want him tagging along with her when she went after Angel. She wished she had Jonathan Crossland with her, though. He was a man who knew what to do.

"I'll go after those three men," Brady told Ellie. "It's my job. I don't want you getting killed."

"I don't think you have to worry about Ellie," Sue said.

She tried to sit up, but Brady put a hand on her shoulder and she lay back.

"You just take it easy for a while," Brady told her. "I don't think the marshal should start back until daylight. Moon ought to be able to last it out till then."

"You're damn right he's able," Moon said. His voice was raspy and weaker than Sue's. "I don't like lyin' here and listenin' to you talk like I'm half dead. I could still whip the lot of you with one hand tied behind me."

Ellie had to laugh. "Mr. Moon, you are a ring-tailed tooter."

"You know it," Moon said. "You don't worry about me, Miss Ellie. You go after those sons of bitches. You know what to do."

Brady Tolbert stood up. "Looks like I'm outvoted," he said.

"You sure as to God are," Moon said. "You leave Shag here with us and you and Miss Ellie go after them three."

Brady looked at Ellie.

"I'm ready when you are," she said. "Soon as I can find my horse."

"Let's go find it, then," Brady said.

Chapter 30

—◦◦◦—

Hoot and Jephson caught up with Angel not far from the church. He didn't seem to be in any hurry.

As they got closer to the river, the trees were thicker, offering plenty of concealment, and the rain was slowing down at last. But there was plenty of other water to worry about. They could all hear the sound of the river rushing over limestone rocks.

"How're we supposed to cross that river?" Hoot asked shakily. "Sounds like we'll wash away if we try."

Hoot didn't want to mention it, because he didn't like to admit it even to himself, but he was afraid of water. Not water like rainwater, but deep water, water that might get over his head and into his mouth and eyes. He wasn't afraid of any man, no matter how big or bad. He wasn't afraid of animals, either, not even of snakes. But he was afraid of water.

It was all because of what had happened to him once when he was a kid. His father said that he was going to teach Hoot to swim, and they'd gone down to the creek that ran through the woods not too far from the back door of the little shack where they lived. Without a word of warning, Hoot's father had picked Hoot up and thrown him right out into the middle of the brackish brown water.

Hoot had sunk straight to the bottom of the creek, his hands sinking into the thick, slimy mud. He'd opened his mouth to yell for help, and the nasty-tasting water filled his throat and choked him. He'd thrashed and tried to cry out, but it was no use. He would have died right then and there if his father hadn't waded into the creek and pulled him out.

When Hoot had finally stopped crying, his father said, "It's swim or sink in this world, you little bastard, and it's all up to you which one you do. Are you ready to go again?"

Hoot knew what would happen to him if he said he wasn't. He could feel the razor strap cutting into his back already.

"I'm ready," he said, and his father threw him in again.

Hoot knew he was going to die, but this time he didn't fight it. He just lay in the mud and let the water flow into his mouth and nose.

His father came for him again, but this time he carried him straight back to the house and beat him. There hadn't been any more swimming lessons after that, and Hoot had avoided any water deeper than an inch or two for the rest of his life to this point.

"A little water won't hurt you," Angel said. "We'll find a place where it's not so bad, and we'll go across there."

Hoot didn't say anything. He nudged the mule forward and hoped there was a bridge somewhere along the way.

Laurie was hoping, too. She was hoping there would come a time when she could slip away from Uncle Angel again.

She'd come to not long after Angel had left the church, but she'd played possum. It wasn't easy to lie still while Angel talked about crossing some river and getting all wet, but he was resting one hand on her back, so she couldn't try anything right then.

She thought she had to try before they got to the river, however. She couldn't swim at all, and the sound of the racing water was enough to discourage even someone who could.

Laurie thought the men were riding along the river-bank now, or not far from it. The sound of the water was a constant roaring. Now and then a tree branch brushed her legs.

She heard Hoot say, "I don't think there's any way to cross. We better just go along like this for a while and then turn back north."

"I don't want to go north," Angel said. "I'm headin' south."

"We can't make any time in these trees," Hoot said. "That woman's gonna get some help and catch up with us."

Laurie knew the woman he was talking about must be Miss Ellie. Laurie had seen her in the trees back at the old church. She couldn't see her very well, but she was sure it had been Miss Ellie. She hadn't been a bit surprised. It was just like Miss Ellie to come and look for her.

"Where's she gonna get any help?" Angel asked.

"We didn't kill ever'body back there. I could hear 'em in the church while you were talkin' to the woman."

"You got right sharp ears, kid," Angel said. "Wonder why they didn't come out and help her while she was standin' there under the gun?"

"Prob'ly because they didn't hear us. Or maybe they were just too busy. They had some wounded to worry about."

"That could be it, all right. Well, if they want to look for us, let 'em come."

Laurie wondered who could have been in the church. Maybe her father had been there. He would have come after her along with Miss Ellie, all right. But Uncle Angel had said that someone was wounded. She hoped it wasn't her father.

"You want 'em to come," Jephson said. "In fact, you want 'em to catch up with us. Ain't that right, Angel?"

"What's that supposed to mean?" Hoot said. "Are you crazy, Jephson? Angel don't want anybody to catch up with us."

"Sure he does," Jephson said. "Ask him."

"You're too smart for your own good, ain't you, Jephson," Angel said.

"You mean he's right?" Hoot said. "You want 'em to catch up with us?"

Jephson's voice was tired. "I finally figgered it out, Hoot. I wondered why Angel didn't seem to be in any big hurry when we left that ranch. It was because he didn't care if someone caught up with us. That's what he wanted all along."

Hoot didn't seem to get it. "What's he talkin' about, Angel? Who do you think's goin' to be after us, anyhow?"

"Somebody named Brady Tolbert," Jephson said.

Laurie almost smiled. Brady was her other uncle. She didn't see him very often, but she liked him. Of course, she'd liked Angel, too, but that was before he'd carried her off from the ranch and lied to her about the picnic. She didn't like Angel at all now.

"Who's Brady Tolbert?" Hoot wanted to know.

Laurie wanted to yell out, "He's a Texas Ranger, and he'll put you all in jail!" But she kept quiet. She even tried not to breathe.

"He's the bastard that put me in the pen," Angel said. "Him and my sister and that husband of hers. I've taken care of two of them. Now it's his turn."

Laurie flinched at that. She couldn't help it.

"I thought you were possumin'," Angel said to her. "You might as well know that your daddy's been shot and your mother's prob'ly dead."

Laurie struggled to sit up. She wanted to hit Angel, to claw his face, to draw his blood.

"You're a liar!" she said. "You're just a great big liar!"

Angel mashed down on her back and held her in place.

"You're practically an orphan," he said. "You can start gettin' used to it. All you got left in the world is your uncle Angel. You and me are gonna live down in Mexico, where folks'll treat us right."

"I don't want to go to Mexico! I want my mother!"

"She won't be comin'. Maybe your uncle Brady will, but me and the boys'll take care of him. I'm gonna be your shield and protection from now on out."

"No, you're not! They won't let you!"

"They can't stop me," Angel said. "Plenty have tried, but it just didn't work out."

"Uncle Brady stopped you."

"You might say that. He stopped me once. But that was just luck. He caught me by surprise. It won't happen again."

"He will too stop you. And if he doesn't, Miss Ellie will."

"Miss Ellie," Angel said. "That the woman I was talkin' to back there at the church?"

Laurie didn't know for sure who Angel had spoken to, but she said, "Yes, and she's going to get you. You wait and see."

Angel laughed. "You think that woman can stop me? She tried once, but she never even pulled a trigger. I don't think we have to worry much about her."

"You'll see," Laurie said. "You'll see."

"I guess we will," Angel said.

PART 3

Chapter 31

"You're sure they went this way?" Brady Tolbert asked.

"I'm sure they were headed this way when they started off," Ellie said. "I can't say that they didn't double back or that they didn't just go on back to town."

"Just checking," Brady said. "Following the river doesn't seem like the smartest thing to do, and it's not like Angel to do something that's not smart."

It had stopped raining about a quarter of an hour earlier. The clouds were thinning out, and the moon was peeping through them now and then, touching their ragged edges with silver-gray light. Ellie had taken off her slicker and stowed it behind the saddle.

She still wasn't sure what to make of Brady Tolbert. He obviously hadn't liked the idea of having her go with him, and he didn't seem to trust her judgment completely, but at the same time he was respectful enough.

"Maybe they're planning to cross the river," Ellie said. "Head south for Mexico."

"You live around here, so you should know about the river. Where can they cross?"

"Now, that's going to be a problem for them. I don't think they can cross it. If that's their plan, they're out of luck. It's been raining hard for hours, and there's no telling how much it rained north and west of here. That river's flowing full and fast enough to sweep away a man and a mule without half trying. And there's no bridge, not around here. It's a long way to a bridge in this direction."

"Angel wouldn't have any way of knowing that, though, would he?"

"I don't know about that," Ellie said. "Maybe he's spent some time in these parts before."

"Maybe. But if he has, he wouldn't be going this way. Not if he was smart."

Ellie was getting a little irritated by the Ranger's insinuations.

"If you want to go off in some other direction," she said, "you're welcome to do it. This is the way I'm going, but you can go wherever you want to."

Brady stopped his horse and leaned on the saddle horn until Ellie had ridden up next to him.

"Kinda touchy, aren't you," he said.

Ellie didn't think of herself as touchy. She thought of herself as pretty even-tempered. But she had to admit that the Ranger had riled her some.

"If I am, it's because those three men have done some things I can't forgive. They tried to kill your brother and your sister-in-law, and they carried off your niece. God only knows what they'll do to her if we don't stop them."

"I didn't say I blamed you. I just said you were touchy."

"You don't think I know what I'm doing."

Brady chuckled. "It's not that. I just can't figure out why Angel's not trying harder to get away from us. What he's doing doesn't make any sense, and that's not like him. He's a little crazy, but he's not stupid. Could be he's trying to lead us into a trap."

Ellie thought about that. Then she said, "He's done one or two other things that don't seem real smart to me."

"What things?"

"Well, taking Laurie, for one. Why would he do that?"

Brady rode along slowly, and for several minutes he didn't say anything.

"I can't figure it," he said finally. "Looks like she'd slow them down. You got any ideas?"

"No. And there's something else."

"What's that?"

"Why did he stop in that old church? If he really wanted to get away, he would've just kept on going. He must've gotten to the church before the river got too high to cross. If he'd gone on ahead, we might never have caught up to him."

"You're right. It's almost like he wanted us to find him. By God, I'll bet he *is* setting a trap."

"You could be right about that," Ellie agreed. "Remember that message I gave you back at the church, that he'd be looking for you?"

Brady said that he remembered.

"Well, that sounds like he's got something in mind for you, all right. It's almost like he's waiting for you."

Once again Brady was quiet for a while as he thought things over. Ellie didn't have any more to say, either, and the only sounds were those made by their horses and the river.

It had turned cool after the rain stopped. The moon was still glowing around the edges of the clouds, and it had started down. Ellie wondered what time it was. Midnight, maybe, or a little after. She didn't care. She'd ride all night and the next day, too, if she could do anything to help Laurie. It galled her that she'd had to let Angel ride off with the girl, but sometimes you had to put aside your feelings and make the best of things. She'd catch up to Angel sooner or later, and she'd get Laurie back from him. That was a promise that she'd made to herself.

Brady broke his silence. "Angel wouldn't have any way of knowing I was here," he said.

Ellie didn't know what he was driving at, and she said so.

"I think he took Laurie to get back at me," Brady told her.

Ellie figured it out then. Everything fell into place.

"I bet you're right," she said. "I thought Sue was dead, and when I told Angel, he said he was sorry he wasn't the one who'd killed her. And he said he hoped he'd get a chance to kill your brother later on. He's out for revenge."

"You sound like you know something about that," Brady said.

"What I know is that it's not all it's cracked up to be. I told Angel that, but it didn't impress him. Sue told me that he's always been of a mind to get back at people he thinks have done him wrong."

"So I've heard. And now he wants to get back at me because I helped put him in prison. It makes sense. He could be pretty sure I'd come for him after I heard about Laurie. What he didn't know was that I was already on the way."

"So he's going to just dawdle along, taking his good time, and wait for you to catch up with him."

"That's the way I see it. But he's going to get fooled. For one thing, I'm a whole lot closer to him than he probably thinks I am."

"That's one thing. Is there anything else?"

"Maybe," Brady said.

"What would it be?"

Brady smiled and looked at Ellie. "He doesn't know I have help."

No, Ellie thought. *That's where you're wrong. He doesn't know that I have help.*

Chapter 32

Laurie hated her uncle Angel now. She hated him for taking her away from her home, she hated him for lying to her, and she hated him for saying that her father had been shot and that her mother was dead.

Her mother wasn't dead. She was sure of it. It didn't matter what Angel said. There were some things that were just too awful to be true, and that was one of them.

She was more determined than ever to get away from Angel and the other men. She was certain that Miss Ellie was coming after her, and maybe her father was too. Maybe he'd been shot, but he wouldn't let that stop him.

And then there was Uncle Brady. He'd be coming as soon as he heard what Angel had done. He was a Texas Ranger, and Laurie knew that the Texas Rangers never failed to get whomever they set out after. Her mother had told her that, and, unlike Uncle Angel, her mother had never lied to her.

She listened to the men talking, waiting for her chance to escape them.

* * *

"What do you think, Hoot?" Angel asked. "Think we could ford the river about here?"

"Good God, no," Hoot responded. "Look at that. We wouldn't have a hope in hell."

"How about it, Jephson. You think Hoot's right?"

"He's right," Jephson agreed. "We better keep on looking."

"All right by me," Angel said. "We can look all night, far's I'm concerned."

As they rode along on the mules, Bob Jephson told himself that he was seven kinds of a fool. Maybe seventy kinds. He'd stayed with Angel because he'd thought Angel was smart. He'd thought Angel would know how to avoid the law and therefore avoid going back to prison.

But Angel didn't seem to give much of a damn whether he went back to prison or not. All he cared about was getting a little of his own back with the people he thought had betrayed him.

As far as Jephson was concerned, the whole idea was crazy. And Jephson certainly hadn't bargained on having a little girl along with them. That made things even worse. She was as likely to get killed as not if shooting broke out on the trail. Angel seemed to care about her, but it apparently hadn't occurred to him that he was putting her in danger. Or if it had occurred to him, he was doing a good job of ignoring it.

And Hoot was just as crazy as Angel. Maybe worse.

There was no telling what he would do to the girl if he got the chance. The only good thing was that he wouldn't get the chance as long as Angel was around.

Or me, Jephson thought. He knew he couldn't let anything happen to the girl, any more than Angel could. It was bad enough that he hadn't tried to stop Hoot from shooting those people back at the church. Probably a couple of them were dead, at the very least. It couldn't go on. If Hoot tried anything with the girl, Jephson knew he'd have to step in and try to stop it.

They had worked their way down as close to the river as they could. In what little moonlight there was, Jephson could see the swirling white-foamed water that raced over the rocky bed and crashed into the stones that stuck up at odd angles all along the way.

A man who got off into water like that would most likely be knocked down within ten seconds and drowned within ten minutes. Or, if he was lucky enough to stay alive, he'd have three or four broken bones to worry him.

"We could make better time if we got away from the river," he said. "We could get back on flat ground and have a lot better chance of gettin' away from here."

"What're you worryin' about?" Angel asked him. "For all we know, there's nobody followin' us. We got all the time in the world."

Jephson didn't disagree, but he was convinced that Angel was wrong. That woman back at the church hadn't looked to Jephson like the kind who gave up easily. Maybe he should've let Hoot shoot her, but he just couldn't do that.

"What about that woman?" he asked.

"You ever hear of a woman that could take on three men with guns?" Angel asked. "I'd hate to think I was a-scared of a woman."

"I'm not scared," Jephson said.

But to tell the truth, he was. A little. There was something about the way she looked.

"What about those people Hoot heard in the church?" he asked.

"They're all shot up," Angel said. "Ain't that right, Hoot."

"That's right," Hoot answered. "Most of 'em, anyway."

"See?" Angel said. "They won't be ridin' anywhere if they're shot. So we don't have to get in any big rush. We're doin' just fine."

"And besides, you want 'em to catch us," Hoot said. "Ain't that what Jephson was tryin' to tell me a while back?"

"That's right," Angel said. "But tell the truth, now, Hoot. You don't care if they catch up to us, do you?"

"Hell, no."

"You'd prob'ly even have yourself a pretty good time, wouldn't you?"

"Could be," Hoot said, and Jephson could tell that he was smiling, though he couldn't see his face. "And it might not be too long now before we find out. Somebody's back there. I can hear 'em."

Jephson couldn't hear a thing above the sound of the river, but when it came to hearing, Hoot hadn't made any mistakes so far.

"Well, then," Angel said. "I guess we'd better make 'em welcome."

"How'll we go about doin' that?" Hoot asked.

Angel looked around. There were several large trees a little farther up the riverbank, and he pointed to them.

"You wait back in there, Hoot. Let 'em ride right on by you. Jephson and I can ride on a little ways. See those big rocks up there?"

He pointed on up the river, and Jephson saw a couple of large white rocks that jutted up out of the ground.

"I see 'em," Hoot said.

"We'll ride on around those rocks and stop. When whoever's comin' rides past you, you can open up. When you start shootin', so will we. You'll be shootin' toward the river, and we'll be shootin' back down along the bank, so there's no danger we'll get in a cross fire."

Jephson knew one thing. He wasn't going to be part of another ambush. The one at the church had been bad enough. But he didn't know how he was going to get away from Angel.

"Let's go," Angel said.

Jephson sat still for a second or two, then flicked the mule's reins and followed Angel up the river.

Chapter 33

Angel and Jephson had hardly concealed themselves behind the rocks when Angel said, "There they come."

Laurie waited until he moved his hand from her back to reach for his pistol. As soon as he did, she sank her teeth into his leg.

He yelped in surprise, and Laurie slipped from his lap. She hit the ground running.

"Miss Ellie!" she called. "Miss Ellie."

Hoot heard her yelling, said, "Damn," and got off a couple of shots at the two people who were now almost directly opposite him.

He missed Ellie, who had urged her horse into a lope as soon as she heard Angel yell, but he hit Brady Tolbert. Tolbert jerked upright and tried to turn and fire, but Angel shot him out of the saddle.

"Get the woman," Angel told Jephson. "I'm going after the girl."

Jephson had no intention of getting the woman. He'd had enough of Angel. It was time for him to strike out on his own, something he should have done a long time ago, and if he got sent back to Huntsville, well, that was just his bad luck. At least in prison he wouldn't have to deal with Angel any longer.

So he just turned his mule around and rode away.

Laurie hadn't gone more than thirty yards before she was completely lost. She hadn't been able to see where they were headed, and all she knew was that she didn't want to run in the direction of the river.

Instead, she'd run the opposite way, but as soon as she'd gotten into the trees and out of Angel's sight, she had no idea where Miss Ellie was. She called out again before she realized that making noise might be a bad idea. Maybe Miss Ellie would hear her, but so would Angel.

She certainly didn't want Angel to hear her, so she stopped calling out and tried to make as little noise as possible. It was quite dark in the trees, so it was hard to be quiet. She kept letting branches swish as they swung back into place after being shoved aside, but at least her bare feet were silent on the ground.

However, she wasn't silent when she stepped on the sharp point of a broken stick. She shouted out in pain and then clapped her hands over her mouth.

But she was too late.

Someone had heard her.

*　*　*

Angel looked back and saw that the woman was riding hard toward the rocks, while that bastard Jephson was headed the other way. Angel had known all along that he couldn't trust Jephson to do the right thing. He would have shot him right then, but he had to deal with the woman first.

He fired a shot but missed. The woman kept right on coming. Angel fired again, missed again. The woman didn't even slow down.

"Goddamn," he said, and then Ellie was on him.

She had her pistol drawn, but she hadn't fired it. She knew she couldn't shoot straight enough to hit anything while she was riding. So she simply headed her horse right at Angel's mule and waited for the collision.

It didn't come, because her horse veered off at the last second, giving Angel the chance to swing his pistol at her head and clip her just behind the ear as she passed by. She almost lost her grip on the reins and slumped forward over the saddle horn. Her horse kept going and was almost at once lost from sight in the trees.

Angel started to go after her and finish her off, but he decided to deal with Jephson first.

"What the hell's goin' on?" Angel said. "I told you to take care of that woman."

"I don't shoot women. And I don't like bein' around people who do."

"Well, ain't that too bad. What makes you feel so high and mighty all of a sudden?"

"It's not sudden," Jephson said. "I've just now got the gumption to tell you how I feel about things."

Angel leveled his pistol on Jephson. "Then I guess I should let you know how I feel, too," he said, and pulled the trigger.

Jephson started to go for his own gun, but it was far too late. The bullet from Angel's Peacemaker tore through Jephson's chest, smashed a chunk out of the left side of his heart, and went right on out his back.

Jephson sat in his saddle for a second, staring at Angel, eyes wide as if he couldn't quite believe what had happened to him. Then his brain got the message that he was dead and he fell backward off the mule. He hit the ground and lay still.

"Never did trust the son of a bitch," Angel said to no one in particular.

He looked around for the woman, but there was no sign of her. He thought he'd better find her. He knew he hadn't hurt her too bad when he hit her with the pistol.

After he found the woman, he'd deal with Laurie. He didn't think she'd be going very far.

Hoot looked down at Laurie. She was holding her hands over her mouth and staring up at him with frightened eyes.

"Hey," Hoot said.

Laurie didn't answer. She kept her hands clasped tightly over her mouth.

"All that shootin's kinda scary, ain't it," Hoot said.

"I'm not scared," Laurie said.

It wasn't true. She was scared, all right. She was just as scared of Hoot as she would if he'd been the Headless Horseman. Maybe even more scared, since the Headless Horseman was just somebody in a story.

Hoot smiled down at her with that smile she didn't like, not one bit.

"I'm glad you ain't scared," he said. "Because I wouldn't want you to be scared of me. I'm the one's gonna help you get out of this mess."

Laurie dropped her hands. "How?"

"Well, Angel's not here right now to boss me around, so I'm gonna do what I want to do instead of what he tells me. And what I want to do is get away from all this water. I don't much like water, myself. What about you?"

"I like water just fine."

Hoot's smile faltered. He said, "All the same, we're gettin' out of here. I'll just reach down and take your hand, and you can swing up behind me."

"I'm not going anywhere with you."

"Sure you are," Hoot said. He showed her the shotgun. "Because if you don't, you'll be scattered all over these woods. See what I mean?"

Laurie saw what he meant. She felt like crying, but she didn't. She told herself that she'd gotten away from Uncle Angel and she could get away from Mr. Hoot, too.

So when he reached out his hand, she reached up and took it.

Hoot pulled her up behind him. "We're gonna find us

a nice dry place," he said, "and then we'll have us a mighty good time. You know what I mean?"

Laurie didn't know. And she didn't want to know.

That didn't bother Hoot. He smiled and urged the mule forward.

Chapter 34

Brady Tolbert couldn't get off the ground. He'd been shot twice, once in the leg and once in the shoulder, and all he could do was lie there and listen to the sound of guns going off.

In only a few seconds, it was quiet again, except for the sound of the rampaging river. He thought he could feel its power shuddering through the bank where he lay.

He had no idea what had happened to Ellie. Or to anyone else. He tried once again to get up, but the pain in his right leg was too intense.

There was another shot. Brady struggled, but he couldn't stand. His horse was only a few yards away. He thought that if he could get the horse to come to him, he might be able to grab hold of a stirrup and pull himself up with one arm. Not his right arm, however. That one was more or less paralyzed from the shoulder down. It was hurting like hell, too. He couldn't decide which hurt worse, the arm or the leg, but then he decided it didn't make any difference. Maybe they both hurt about the same.

After a few minutes, he gathered his resources and managed to get himself into a sitting position. His shoulder didn't seem to be bleeding too much, but he thought he'd better do something about his leg. He didn't want to bleed to death. He pulled off his belt and tied it above the wound. It wasn't easy, but he managed by using his left hand and his teeth.

The wound, to tell the truth, wasn't bleeding as much as he'd feared. It seemed like he'd gotten off lucky. Just a few hunks of flesh torn away. Nothing that was going to kill him. It was just going to hurt enough to make him feel like it was killing him. But he could deal with that.

It had been a while, and there still hadn't been any more shooting. Angel must have killed Ellie back in those rocks, Brady thought, and that made him feel even worse than his wounds. His vision blurred, and he felt suddenly dizzy. He almost let himself lie back down, but he didn't. He stayed upright until the dizziness passed.

When it did, he called his horse, which looked at him with idle curiosity and then looked away. He called again, and tried whistling. The whistle came out like a long, low breath. His lips were too dry. He licked them and tried again. This time he got out a weak semblance of a whistle, and the horse's ears perked up.

"Come on over here, you bay son of a bitch," Brady said.

The horse looked at him for a while, then walked slowly over.

"I'm sorry I cussed you," Brady said, reaching for the stirrup.

It took him a couple of minutes, but he managed to pull himself upright without biting through his bottom lip or passing out. He was sweating heavily, and he didn't think he had much chance of getting into the saddle. But he had to try.

Maybe he'd better loosen the belt first. Didn't want to get gangrene in his leg.

When he untied his makeshift tourniquet, he found that the bleeding had stopped. That was good news. He wished he had some whiskey to pour on the wound, but he didn't.

To put his left foot in the stirrup, he'd have to stand on his right leg, which didn't seem too likely. Well, it had to be done. If he hung on to the saddle horn, he wouldn't have to put much weight on the leg. And if he moved really fast, maybe he could get in the saddle without fainting.

He took a deep breath, said, "Here we go," and gave it a try.

Ellie had been momentarily stunned by the blow from Angel's pistol, but her hat and her hair had protected her from any serious damage. She got control of her horse and reined it in just as she heard a pistol shot from Angel's direction.

Tolbert? Maybe. But then again, maybe not. She knew he'd been shot. She didn't think he'd be coming to help her.

She sat and listened. There were no more shots. She turned her horse and started cautiously back toward where she'd last seen Angel.

She wondered where Laurie was. She'd heard her call out, but for the second time that night, she hadn't been able to do anything to help her. It was infuriating, although she knew it wasn't her fault. Still, it made her feel bad.

As she looked for Angel, she tightened her grip on her pistol. She didn't care whether she hit him or not; this time she was by God going to shoot him. Or at least shoot *at* him.

She listened but didn't hear anyone coming in her direction, and she got a little careless. She hadn't thought Angel might simply be waiting for her.

But as soon as she rode past a particularly large tree, she heard his voice behind her.

"You've sure been a powerful trouble to me, lady," he said.

She turned as fast as she could and pulled the trigger of her Peacemaker twice.

The first shot ripped away about three inches of the trunk of the tree beside which Angel was sitting on his mule.

The second sent Angel's hat flying backward into the darkness.

Angel was taken completely by surprise. He'd never met up with a woman like this one before, a woman who'd just start shooting at you without a word of warning. It was just the kind of thing he would have done. In fact, it was exactly what he *should* have done. But it sure wasn't right for a woman to do it.

Ellie continued to pull the trigger. Her third shot took off the top of Angel's mule's left ear.

The mule jerked like a galvanized frog, then sprang forward at a dead run, or what passed for it. Angel was yanked backward, and when he straightened up, a tree limb almost took off his head. He ducked just in time, and when he looked up again he saw that he was headed straight for the river.

He hauled back hard on the reins, but the mule paid no attention. Drops of blood from his ear flew back and hit Angel in the face.

"Whoa, you hammerheaded bastard!" Angel yelled, but that didn't help, either. Angel might as well have been trying to stop a runaway locomotive.

The mule hit the edge of the rushing water and managed to go two more steps before it was knocked off balance and went down. The current dragged it almost under, and Angel along with it. Angel let go of the reins and kicked his feet out of the stirrups to avoid being pulled down.

The cold river tumbled Angel over once or twice,

and he lost his pistol and his hat. Water filled his eyes and nose, and he kicked hard to avoid the mule that was windmilling nearby. Then the mule shot off on down the river. Angel flailed his arms in an attempt to keep his head above water.

He succeeded, but his head made a tempting target. Ellie shot at it. The bullet hit the water well to Angel's right.

Ellie shot again. This time the bullet hit a bit closer, but Angel was being pulled downstream so quickly that he was out of range before she could reload and take another shot.

The water was full of sticks and limbs, but not a one that would do him any good. They were all too small.

Except for the tree trunk that was bearing down on him atop the white foam that glistened in the scant moonlight.

Angel banged off a rock and almost went under again. The log didn't hit the rock and didn't slow down. It was heading straight for Angel's head.

Ellie watched from the edge of the river as the water carried Angel farther and farther away. If it hadn't been for his nearly white hair, his head would have been just a distant black blob on the even blacker water.

It appeared to Ellie that the log was going to strike him, and she was angered that he was escaping her. She should have been the one to punish him for what he'd done to Lane and Sue and Laurie.

But when his head disappeared in front of the log, she told herself that she was no better than he was, that she was interested only in getting back at the one who'd hurt her. She knew that doing so wouldn't really matter in the long run.

What mattered was Laurie, and Ellie had to find her.

Chapter 35

Hoot heard the distant pistol shots and laughed. He was feeling good. No one was shooting at him. He had the girl, he was well away from the river, and he was going back to the church house to get dry.

He knew there might still be someone in the church, but that didn't bother him. He figured they were all shot up, or, if they weren't, they would be as soon as he got there. He patted the sawed-off shotgun. There wasn't anybody who could stand up against that, no matter who they were.

And he had the girl. He liked her a lot. She was spunky and cute, and she made him think about things he hadn't much considered since he got out of prison. The other three men—Jephson, Angel, and Abilene Jack Sturdivant—had got them a whore as soon as they could, but Hoot hadn't been interested. He couldn't really say why. But he was interested now, all right. Had been, ever since he'd seen the girl.

He couldn't do anything about her with Angel around, not with Angel acting like he was her daddy, but

Angel was behind Hoot now, and Hoot was just as glad he was. He had no idea what was happening to Angel, and he didn't give a damn. Hoot had been getting pretty tired of the way Angel was ordering him around, even telling him not to cuss in front of the girl.

"Shit," he said aloud. "I can cuss anytime I want to. Nobody can tell me not to. Ain't that right, Laurie."

There was no answer, and Hoot said, "Laurie. That's your name, ain't it, honey? Speak up, now."

Laurie's voice was low. "That's my name."

"That's right. I knew it was, so you'd just as well own up to it. You like old Hoot, don't you?"

Laurie didn't say anything.

Hoot laughed. He said, "You're a shy one, ain't you? But that don't bother me, not one little bit. I like a girl that ain't too outspoken. It's not becomin' for a girl to talk too much."

Laurie didn't respond.

Hoot wasn't bothered. Let her keep quiet. That was all to the good as far as he was concerned. He could carry on a conversation with no one at all if he had to.

"We're goin' back to that church," he said. "You'll like it there this time. You'll see."

"Miss Ellie won't let you do anything to me," Laurie said. "My daddy won't, either."

"I can't say for sure about Miss Ellie, but I wouldn't be expectin' any help from her if I was you. I imagine a couple of those shots we heard back there put paid to her bill, if you take my meanin'."

"You're just like Uncle Angel. You think you know everything. But you don't know Miss Ellie. She won't let anything happen to me, and neither will my daddy."

"Your daddy's dead as a doornail back there at that ranch," Hoot said. "And Angel's most likely filled your Miss Ellie full of lead. You can forget about them."

Laurie opened her mouth, but no words came out. She felt hot tears in her eyes.

I'm not going to cry, she told herself. *I'm going to get away, just like I got away from Uncle Angel, and Miss Ellie will come for me.*

Hoot started to sing "Jesus Loves Me."

Laurie had been taught that Jesus loved everyone. For the first time, she wondered if that was really true. She didn't see how anyone could love Hoot, not even Jesus.

Brady Tolbert saw the rider coming out from the rocks, and he knew at once it was Ellie Taine, unless Angel had killed her and traded his mule for her horse.

But that hadn't happened. It was Ellie, all right, and she looked at him with concern as she came up to him.

"I thought you were killed," she said.

"I almost am, but I'll live. And I can ride." He didn't bother to mention how much he was hurting and how much he just wanted to find a place where he could lie down and go to sleep. "What happened in there?"

"I lost Laurie. I shot the ear off Angel's mule, and the mule took off into the river."

"That's mighty good shooting."

Ellie smiled. "I didn't mean to shoot the ear off. I was shooting at Angel."

"I guess you don't shoot as good as I thought, then."

"I don't shoot so well at all. Sometimes I can hit what I aim at, though."

"I'll bet you can. What happened to Angel in the river?"

"I hope he drowned. The mule pitched him off, and it looked like a big log hit him square in the head. I didn't see him again after that."

"Maybe we won't have to worry about him, then. What about Laurie?"

"She must've gotten away from Angel. She might be back in the trees, but I called for her and didn't get an answer."

"There were two other men with Angel."

"There's only one now. The other one's back there on the ground."

"You get him?"

"No. I think it must've been Angel."

"I wouldn't be surprised," Brady said. "He's mean enough to kill his own partners, that's for sure. Which one was it?"

"It looked like the one called Jephson."

"Which means Hoot's still around. You think he has Laurie?"

"Yes." Ellie's voice shook just the slightest bit. "But I don't know which way he's headed."

"We'll find out."

"How?"

"Well," Brady said, "I figure that if Jephson's dead back in the rocks, then Hoot must be the one who shot me from those trees. That's where we'll start."

They rode over to the trees. Every step that Brady's horse took caused pain to lance through his leg and shoulder. He gritted his teeth and tried to smile. Sweat broke out on his forehead.

They found where Hoot's horse had stood. It wasn't hard to follow him from there, even in the dark. He wasn't being careful, and he'd broken limbs when they got in his way. It wasn't long before they located the place where Hoot had found Laurie.

"Look here," Brady said through clenched teeth. "I believe he's turned around and headed back."

It looked that way to Ellie, too.

"Where do you think he's going?" she asked.

"Back to the church, maybe," Brady said. "I don't know why he'd do that, though."

"He might not know anyone's still there," Ellie said. "He might think it'd be the last place we'd look for him."

"Well, he'd be wrong about that, wouldn't he," Brady said.

"Do you think you can make it back there?" Ellie asked.

"I can make it."

"You don't look like it."

"Lady, I've seen men hurt worse than I am walk ten miles while they were carrying a saddle on their backs."

"I hope you don't think I believe you."

"I didn't think you would. But you don't need to worry about me. I'll be fine."

"I guess we'll see about that."

"I guess we will," Brady said.

Chapter 36

━━◆━═╪═━◆━━

As he neared the church, Hoot heard an owl off in the distance.

"Owl's been huntin'," he said. "Got him a rabbit, prob'ly."

Laurie said she didn't care.

"I don't blame you. Rabbits don't matter much when you think about it."

The moon was nearly down, and Hoot figured it must be around two or three o'clock in the morning. He stopped his mule and listened. He couldn't hear anything at the church, but he could see that there were some horses out front. There was no light inside.

"Guess they're all asleep," he said. "I kinda hate to wake 'em up."

He didn't hate it at all. He was looking forward to it, no matter how many of them there were. He counted four horses. If they were from the same bunch that he'd met up with earlier, he knew he'd shot three of them. Maybe they weren't dead, but they weren't going to be dancing any jigs, either. He figured that with the shotgun and the pistol, he had the advantage on them.

Except, of course, for the girl. He had to do something with the girl, and he already knew that she had a habit of yelling out when she got the chance. So he wouldn't give her the chance. He turned the mule and rode into the trees.

When he got well away from the church, he said, "We're gonna rest here for a while."

"I thought you said we were going to the church."

"We are. But we're gonna rest first."

Hoot swung down from the saddle and reached up for Laurie, who immediately lunged the other way. She slipped off the mule and hit the ground running.

She might have escaped, but Hoot was too quick for her. She got no more than a couple of steps from the mule before he caught up with her.

"I was afraid you'd try something like that," he said. "Now I'm gonna have to tie you up."

Laurie struggled and tried to jerk away. She opened her mouth to scream, but Hoot slapped a hand over it.

"I knew you'd try that, too," he said.

He hoisted her writhing, kicking body under his arm, keeping one hand over her mouth, and carried her to the mule.

"I'm gonna move my hand now," he said. "If you yell, I'll have to hit you."

Laurie didn't yell. Hoot pulled his wet bandanna from around his neck and stuffed it in her mouth.

"That prob'ly don't taste too good, but it's what you get for yellin'. Now I'll have to tie you up."

He rummaged in a saddlebag until he found a piece of rope. Then he carried Laurie to the nearest tree and tied her to the trunk.

"Don't you go runnin' off while I'm gone," he said when he was finished.

Laurie tried to say something, but the bandanna muffled her voice.

"Don't you worry about bein' out here by yourself, Laurie. Nothin' will bother you, and I'll be back before too long. Then we'll have us a time."

He gave her what he thought was a reassuring grin and left her there.

Laurie waited until Hoot was out of sight before she started struggling with the rope. He had shoved her hard against the tree when he tied her, but she had taken a deep breath and tried to expand her chest. When she let all the air out, she thought she could detect a slight loosening in her bonds.

While she contended with the rope, she also tried to push the gag from her mouth with her tongue. It was wedged in too tightly for her to do much with it. She told herself that she would take it out just as soon as she got free from the rope. Then she would call Miss Ellie. She knew Miss Ellie wasn't dead, no matter what Hoot had said. Miss Ellie was still looking for her, and she'd come to find her.

The rough bark of the tree scratched Laurie's back, and it was tearing her nightgown, but she didn't let that bother her. She was going to get away, and that was all she allowed herself to think about.

Hoot stopped the mule about fifty yards from the church and looped the reins around a tree branch. The four horses were still in the churchyard.

Hoot checked the shotgun to make sure it was loaded. He figured that if the people inside the church were sleeping, he could just walk through the door and kill them before they woke up, two of them with the shotgun and two more with his pistol.

It was going to be messy, but that didn't bother Hoot in the least. It would probably bother Laurie, though, and Hoot didn't like that. He didn't want to get her upset. Maybe he could get whoever was in the building to come outside. That way things wouldn't be quite so bad.

In fact, it would be better if they came out the back door. That way, there wouldn't be anything for Laurie to see when Hoot returned with her.

He started to circle the church, going through the little cemetery. The moon was almost down, and the headstones were black lumps sticking out of the ground. Some of them leaned at crazy angles, and some had tumbled over. Hoot was careful not to trip over them. He didn't give a thought to whoever might be resting beneath the ground. As far as he was concerned, the dead had nothing to say to the living.

When he got to the back of the church, he felt around on the ground until he came up with a couple of small rocks. Then he threw them at the door. They made two solid thumps and bounced away.

Hoot grinned and picked up another rock.

Shag Tillman had been drowsing, back against the wall, but the noise brought him instantly awake. He looked around the dark interior of the church. He could see the shadowy shapes of Harry Moon and Sue Tolbert. Both of them were sleeping soundly. Harry was snoring gently, but that wasn't what Shag had heard.

Fred Willis's body was on the other side of the church. He wasn't likely to have made any noise.

There was another thud against the back door. Somebody was outside. Shag didn't really want to see who it was.

On the other hand, he didn't know that he had much choice. He stood up and checked his pistol. Then he pulled off his boots. He didn't want to make any more noise crossing the floor than he had to. Maybe it was just Ellie Taine out there, or the Ranger, but Shag didn't think so. They wouldn't be tapping on the door. They'd just come on inside.

Shag wished he was back in Blanco, asleep in his own bed. He wished he'd never taken the marshal's job. He hadn't counted on getting into such a mess as this one, where he'd most likely have to use his gun.

Shag didn't much like his chances in any kind of a gunfight. It wasn't that he couldn't shoot. He could shoot all right. He wasn't any sharpshooter, but he could hit what he aimed at most of the time.

Trouble was, what he'd always aimed at was nothing more than a prickly pear or a jackrabbit now and then. He'd never pulled a trigger on anybody who could shoot back, and he didn't want to have to start now.

Unfortunately, there wasn't anybody else around to do it for him. One of the others was dead, and the other two might as well be for all the good they could do him.

Too bad Ellie Taine wasn't there. She had enough gumption for the both of them. She wouldn't mind one bit being in the fix Shag was in. Well, she wasn't there, and that was just the way it was. Shag had already admitted to himself that night that he was a damn coward, but at least he'd come back to the church. Now he was just going to have to go over to that door and see who was outside.

Or maybe there wasn't anyone out there now. Maybe he'd been hearing things. Maybe he could just settle down and go on back to drowsing.

There was another thump on the door.

Damn, Shag thought.

He started across the floor of the church, sliding his feet along, trying not to make a sound. When he reached the door, he stood to one side of it, his back to the wall, and jerked it open.

Chapter 37

‒‒⊫◆⊨‒‒

As soon as the door came open, Hoot fired both barrels of the shotgun before he realized there wasn't anyone standing in the doorway.

"Goddamn," he said, and then he heard horses.

Turning, he saw two riders coming out of the trees and heading toward him. He looked back at the church.

Shag Tillman was standing in the doorway now, and he fired a shot that ricocheted off the ground at Hoot's feet and whined away into the darkness.

Hoot cursed himself for having worried about making a mess in the church. He cursed himself for having left the mule so far away.

He dropped the shotgun and drew his pistol, taking a couple of quick shots at Shag, hoping to give him something to think about if not kill him, and then he started running through the graveyard, jumping over the stones that were in his way.

The two riders were firing at him now, and Hoot

could hear the bullets whizzing by. One of them chipped off a chunk of gravestone and sent it flying into his cheek.

His head jerked aside, and he took his eyes off the stones. The next thing he knew, he was flying through the air.

He landed on his stomach, slid a few yards, then sat up, firing his pistol at the riders.

And laughing. Damn, but he was having fun.

Something slammed into his side, knocking him over against one of the tombstones. Hoot righted himself and fired again and again. He kept right on pulling the trigger even after the hammer was clicking on empty cylinders, and he kept right on laughing.

Shag Tillman waited until the shooting had stopped before he went outside. His knees were a little weak, but he couldn't help that. He wasn't used to being shot at. He was careful to look around the corner of the church before he revealed himself to whoever was out there.

"Is that you, Miss Ellie?" he said.

"It's me," Ellie answered from the graveyard. "Are you all right, Shag?"

"I'm not hit. But I think I winged somebody before you rode up." Shag knew he hadn't winged anyone, but he thought he might as well try to make himself look as good as possible. "Is he out there?"

"He's here, and he's down. Come on over here and help me with Mr. Tolbert."

Shag stepped around the corner. He could see that the Ranger was sagging in his saddle, about to fall. Miss Ellie was standing by her horse, looking down at someone.

"Who's that on the ground?" Shag asked.

"The one they call Hoot. He's been shot in the side and the chest, but he's alive. Don't worry about him. Help Mr. Tolbert into the church."

Tolbert looked just about done in to Shag, but the Ranger said, "I can make it all right."

"You let Shag help you," Ellie said. "I'll take care of this one."

She was holding a shotgun, and she nudged Hoot none too gently with the barrel. Shag was glad he wasn't in Hoot's place right about now.

"Where's Laurie?" Ellie asked.

Hoot didn't answer, and Ellie jabbed him in the chest with the shotgun barrel.

Hoot moaned.

"Don't kill him," Brady Tolbert said. "Then you'll never find the girl."

"I'm not going to kill anybody," Ellie told him. "But he might wish he was dead before long."

Shag helped Brady off the horse. The Ranger could hardly stand. He had to lean heavily on Shag.

"Come on," Shag said to him. "Let's get you inside."

"I'm not going anywhere just yet. Not until I find out where Laurie is."

Hoot made a noise that was halfway between a moan and a laugh.

"Well, you ain't gonna find out from me," Hoot said. He paused, coughed, and then continued. "I'm the only one that knows, and I ain't tellin'."

"You'll tell," Ellie assured him. She jabbed him again with the shotgun.

"Ahhhhhh," Hoot said. "That hurts. But it feels kinda good, too. Do it again."

Ellie took a step backward, and Hoot started laughing.

"The son of a bitch is crazy," Shag said. "Pardon my language, Miss Ellie."

"Let me talk to him," Brady said.

Shag helped the Ranger walk a little closer to Hoot. Brady looked down and said, "Listen, Hoot, I'm a Texas Ranger. I can't make you any promises, but the law might go a little easier on you if you tell us where the girl is."

Hoot choked off his laughter. "The hell with the law. I'm not gonna live long enough to have anything to do with the law. As far as I'm concerned, that little girl can die out there in the woods."

"She's out in the woods, then?" Ellie said.

"Did I say that? I don't rightly remember where she is. Maybe I threw her in the river."

"You didn't go anywhere near that river," Ellie said. "Shag, get Mr. Tolbert inside and then go look in those woods over there. Find the mule this man was riding, and then try to backtrack it."

"What about you?" Shag asked.

Ellie looked at the man on the ground.

"I'll see if I can help Hoot remember any better while you're looking," she said.

By wriggling up and down against the tree trunk, Laurie had managed to loosen the rope so much that it finally slipped down below her waist. When that happened, she was able to get her arms loose, remove the gag from her mouth, and throw it on the ground. Then she forced the ropes down to her feet.

She stepped away from the tree and stood quietly for a moment, trying to get her bearings. That was when the shooting started. Laurie knew it must be coming from the church, and she started to run in that direction.

Within a few minutes she burst out of the trees not far from where Hoot had tied the mule. There was no shooting now, and Laurie could see the little church with the horses in front. And she could see someone in the cemetery.

It was still dark, but Laurie knew immediately who the person was.

"Miss Ellie!" she yelled. "Miss Ellie."

Ellie looked up and saw Laurie running toward her.

"I don't guess I'll be needing your help, after all," she told Hoot.

"Goddammit," Hoot said. "Nothin' ever works out for me." He groaned. "But at least I won't live to go back to that prison."

"You'll be fine," Ellie said. "You might hurt for a while, but you won't die, and you'll go back to prison for sure."

"Goddammit," Hoot said, but Ellie had turned away.

"Here I am, Laurie," she called. "Here I am."

In seconds, Laurie was in her arms.

Chapter 38

Angel dragged himself out of the river and lay on the bank. He'd managed to grab hold of the log and let it give him a ride until it had hung up in the rocks not fifty yards from the church. The water was shallow enough there for Angel to get to the bank without being pulled under again, and after he got his wind back, he stood up and took stock.

He was soaked through, and his clothes clung to him so that it was hard to move. His hair was plastered around his face. He didn't have his pistol, he didn't have his mule, he didn't even have his hat. He sat down and shoved his hair out of his eyes. Then he took off his boots and poured the water out. Reaching into his right boot, he discovered that he still had his knife. He hefted it in his hand, liking the feel and the weight of it.

When the shooting started at the church, Angel flopped on his stomach. He saw the two riders coming out of the trees and cursed under his breath. That damned Brady Tolbert was still alive. And the woman was with him.

He saw that they were firing at someone who was running near the church. Hoot. It had to be Hoot, who, as Angel watched, fell to the ground. He was up on his knees and shooting immediately, but then he was hit and down again.

Looked like it was all over for Hoot, not that Angel really cared. Hoot hadn't been a hell of a lot of help to Angel earlier, and it was clear that he hadn't felt enough loyalty to Angel to try to find out what had happened to him.

Angel waited to see what would happen. One of the riders dismounted, and a man came out of the church. There was some talk that Angel couldn't hear, and the Ranger was helped off his horse. Soon after that, he and the other man went back to the church. The woman stayed with Hoot.

Then Angel heard Laurie calling out to the woman, who turned to her with open arms. Angel squeezed the handle of his knife. It was time for him to make his play.

He covered the ground between himself and the cemetery in a crouching run. No one saw him. The woman was too busy hugging the girl, and Hoot was lying down.

When Angel reached the first gravestones, he knelt behind the largest one. He tried to figure out just exactly where Hoot was. He couldn't have been too far away from the woman's horse, so Angel duckwalked in that direction.

He found Hoot easily. Hoot must've heard him coming, because he was looking straight at him. Hoot had been shot, but his hearing hadn't been affected.

Angel put a finger to his lips, and Hoot gave a slight nod that Angel hardly noticed. His attention was on the woman and the girl.

"They told me they killed my daddy," Laurie was saying.

"They were lying," Ellie said. "Your daddy's going to be just fine."

"What about my mother? Uncle Angel says she's dead."

"Your uncle's a liar. Your mother is just fine, and she's waiting for you inside the church."

Angel slithered over to Hoot and put his mouth next to Hoot's ear.

"Where's your mule?" he asked.

"Over yonder," Hoot whispered. "Some old man's gonna be lookin' for it any minute now."

"I'll get there first."

"You gonna take me with you?"

"Sure," Angel said.

Hoot grinned.

"You shouldn't have run off with my niece, though," Angel said.

"You know how it is," Hoot told him.

"Yeah. I know. And I think I've changed my mind."

"Thought you might," Hoot said, the grin still plastered on his face. "Don't guess it matters much now."

"Don't guess it does," Angel said. "Not to you."

Hoott was still grinning when Angel brought his knife around and slit Hoot's throat from one side to the other, slicing through both carotid arteries and sending blood jetting across the cemetery.

Angel paid no attention to the blood. He was up and running toward Laurie and the woman. Hoot must've made some kind of noise, because they half turned toward Angel, who hit the woman in the chest with his shoulder. She sat down hard.

Angel scooped Laurie up under his arm and kept right on running without looking back. He was about halfway to the trees when the woman yelled for him to stop.

Angel didn't pay her any mind. He knew the woman wouldn't shoot, not as long as he was holding Laurie, who was screaming, kicking, and trying to bite him. He just squeezed her even tighter.

He found the mule with no trouble at all, but he knew he was going to have problems with Laurie. He wasn't sure he could mount the mule without at least a little co-operation from his niece.

"If you'll hold still," he told her, "I won't have to hurt you. If you don't, I'll hit you."

Laurie kept right on struggling. It was as if she hadn't heard him.

"All right," he said. "But remember, this is all your fault."

He was about to club her in the head with the handle of his knife when he heard someone behind him.

"Don't you dare hit her," Ellie said. "If you do, I'll kill you."

Angel turned and saw Ellie standing there, breathing hard and holding the shotgun ready to fire.

Angel smiled at her. "You shoot at me with that thing and you'll kill the both of us. I don't think you want to do that."

Ellie's shoulders slumped, and Angel knew he had her buffaloed. He looked past her and saw someone else coming toward them.

"You tell your friend to keep his distance," Angel said. "Much as I'd hate to hurt this little girl, I'll cut her if you give me a reason."

Laurie kicked and screamed, and Ellie turned her head to see who was coming. It was Shag Tillman. Ellie knew Shag wouldn't be any help to her.

Angel put the point of the knife to the side of Laurie's neck.

"You better calm yourself," he told the girl. "If you don't, this knife might just slide right through your skin."

Laurie stopped kicking.

"That's better," Angel told her. Then he said to Ellie, "Now, I'm gonna get on this mule and ride away from here. You can tell Brady and my sister that I'll have to finish the job on them later. In the meantime, they can think about how happy Laurie's goin' to be with her uncle Angel."

He bent his head down closer to Laurie. "Ain't that right, honey? You really do like your uncle Angel, don't you?"

"No," Laurie said, and she threw her head back and smashed it into Angel's nose.

Angel let out a yelp and dropped Laurie. She hit the ground and rolled, and Angel made a dive at her with the knife. When he did, Ellie pulled the first trigger of the shotgun.

The buckshot hit Angel at about his waist and nearly ripped him in two. A couple of pellets also hit the mule, which brayed and shied away. Angel toppled toward it, missed, and fell to the ground.

"Good God a'mighty," Shag said.

Chapter 39

A week later, Shag was sitting in the swing in Ellie's front yard. Brady Tolbert was in a chair nearby, his shoulder swathed in bandages. Both men were drinking lemonade from glasses that were cool to the touch, though to tell the truth Shag would've preferred something a little stronger than lemonade. It was late afternoon, and a soft breeze was blowing.

"That Angel Ware was ridin' a desperate trail," Shag said. "He must've been a little bit crazy to go up against Ellie Taine."

"I don't think he knew what he was getting into," Brady said.

Shag had to smile at that. "Plenty of men would be fooled, I guess. And by the time they figure out what they've got into, it's too late."

Shag was just glad that Ellie had been there to take care of things. Nothing against the Texas Rangers, but it was easy to see who'd taken control of the situation at the abandoned church. If Shag had to pick somebody to be on his side in a fight, he'd go with Ellie Taine every time.

"Thing is," he said to Brady, "Ellie don't have any idea just how tough she is. She's a hell of a woman."

"That she is," Brady said.

Ellie came out of the house and walked toward them. Sue and Laurie were with her. Ellie was carrying a pitcher of lemonade on a tray.

"Can anyone use another drink?" she asked when she reached them.

"It's mighty good," Shag said, "but I think I've had my limit."

He set his glass on the tray she extended to him.

"What about you, Mr. Tolbert?" she asked.

"I wish you'd call me Brady," he said.

Ellie blushed. Familiarity with men didn't come easy to her.

"As much as we've been through together," Brady said, "you'd think we could call each other by our first names."

"She's Miss Ellie," Laurie said, in case Brady didn't know. "But you can call her Ellie if you want to. She won't mind."

"Now, Laurie," her mother cautioned. "Don't go meddling in other folks' business."

Brady set his glass on the tray. "How about it, Ellie? I've been staying in your house for a week now."

"Well, I guess it's all right," Ellie said. "Brady."

"When will you be headin' back to Del Rio?" Shag asked the Ranger.

"Soon. Maybe tomorrow."

"Oh, no, Uncle Brady," Laurie said. "You have to stay another day. Miss Ellie is going to let me read you a story by Mr. Irving from one of her books. It's about a headless horseman."

"I guess I could stay long enough for that," Brady said. "But my job here's finished, and I'm healed up enough to ride. I have to get back to the Ranger station."

"Before you leave, I wish you'd talk to Miss Ellie about bein' my deputy," Shag said. "I could use a little help in the job."

"Don't go starting that with me again," Ellie told him. "I have a ranch to run. I don't have time to be doing anything else."

"You had time to go off after Angel," Shag pointed out.

"That was different. That was personal."

"There's lots of folks need help besides just the ones you know," Shag said. "What about them?"

"That's your job, I guess," Ellie said.

She'd had no intention of ever getting involved with manhunting or violence again after her first experience. That had been personal, too, but at the same time it had been different. Not that she could explain even to herself what the difference was.

"I'm not real good at the job," Shag said. "Much as I hate to admit it."

"You're better than you think you are. You took on Hoot back at that church. You came out to help me with Angel."

"You didn't need much help with him."

It was true. Ellie knew well enough that she could take care of herself in nearly any situation. That was one thing she'd learned after her husband's death.

But she didn't want to involve herself with other people's troubles, and she didn't want to have to kill anyone else, even if the one she killed was as bad as Angel. Angel had proved to her just how futile it was to go out for revenge, and wasn't that what Shag was really talking about? Justice never seemed to enter into it.

"You know why it is, don't you?" Shag said.

"Why *what* is?" Ellie asked.

"Why you didn't need much help with Angel."

"No. But I have a feeling you're going to tell me."

"I sure enough am. It's because you ain't afraid of the devil. You'd spit in his eye."

Ellie considered. Maybe it was true, though she'd never thought of herself as being particularly brave. She couldn't remember a single time during her pursuit of Angel that she'd felt fear. But that didn't make any difference. She wasn't going to spend her life hunting people down, and that's what she told Shag.

"I don't blame you a bit," Sue Tolbert said. "That's no way to live."

"Somebody has to do it," Brady said.

"I wasn't talking about you. It's your job. Besides, you're a man."

"If you think that makes any difference, you don't know Ellie very well," Brady said.

Sue looked at Ellie.

"Maybe I don't," she said. "But I do know that I have to go look in on Lane and Harry Moon. I thought they were going to have a fight after their last game of checkers."

"Harry needs to get back to work," Shag said. "He never was one to sit around for very long."

"I'll have both of them back in the saddle soon enough," Ellie said. "That's my job. Being the boss of this ranch. Come on, Sue. Let's go see if those checker players want any of this lemonade."

"Maybe I could read them a story," Laurie said, taking her mother's hand and following Ellie back toward the house.

Shag watched them go.

"You ever see another woman like that one?" he asked.

Brady smiled a slow, speculative smile.

"To tell you the truth," he said, "I don't believe I ever did."